"*The Signal* takes us into terrain that's stunning and terrible. In doing so, it becomes both an elegy to a broken marriage and a heart-stopping, suspenseful thriller. It's a difficult journey, but relax: with Ron Carlson, you really are in expert hands."   —*The New York Times Book Review*

"Carlson never drops an extra word or a false phrase, even as *The Signal* accelerates like an avalanche, suspicion rolling into fear and then roaring down with a conclusion that shakes the ground. If men can't be brought back to fiction by books as fine as this one, it's their own damn fault."
—*The Washington Post*

"Ron Carlson's new novel is a love story and a wilderness adventure that mounts to a climax of shocking, and satisfying, violence. . . . Carlson paces his tale with craft and care, never hurrying. *The Signal* is about broken innocence and how, for the individual at least, balance might be found again. Carlson's a romantic—even when he's writing about failings, folly, and violence. This novel . . . has a lingering elegance and power. Lives go wrong, *The Signal* says, but they can be repaired too, if we find our centers and attend to what's around us."
—*Los Angeles Times*

"Read Ron Carlson's latest, *The Signal*, and you'll be convinced that the answer to your worries resides in the woods, in getting back to the basics. . . . It's a sweet, tidy little book about a broken rancher. And yet it won't just help you pass the time, it will help you out."   —*Esquire*

"Long revered as a master of the short story, Carlson has a talent for describing landscape (both internal and external), and that translates here intact. At fewer than two hundred pages, it's beach ready, too."   —*GQ*

"Carlson's new novel comes two years after his wonderful *Five Skies*, and like it, this one depends mightily on the beauty of a rugged place."
—*The Arizona Republic*

"Ron Carlson is probably the best American writer you've never heard of. Carlson's stories and novels are superb, taking as their subject, generally, the psyche of the American man and the dignity of hard work. And his brilliant new novel, *The Signal*, is a landscape portrait of Wyoming, a paean to camping, and a wound-up little thriller all in one. If you're new to Carlson, here's the way to get acquainted."
—*The Daily Beast*

"Carlson excels at articulating the inner life of men who don't talk a whole lot, and his love of the short-story format means that he's not inclined to use twenty words where one will do just fine. *The Signal* offers Carlson's sure-handed, stripped-down prose (I loved his description of fishing flies as 'like a fabulous meeting of jewelry and semi-conductors'); a deep love of nature . . . And unlike a lot of manly-men writers (I'm talking to you, Hemingway), Carlson seems to have a genuine appreciation of women."
—Yvonne Zipp, *The Christian Science Monitor*

"Powerful . . . a bittersweet love story and a rousing adventure set in the remote stretches of the Wind River range of Wyoming, where a couple has planned their tenth annual backpacking trip. . . . Carlson evokes the rugged solace of nature with grace and simplicity, his unadorned prose reminiscent of Cormac McCarthy's. He's as adept at describing the stark beauty of the wild as he is at reflecting the contradictory nature of human interaction. And on the treacherous ground between passion and sentimentality, he never loses his footing."   —*The Miami Herald*

"Uncommonly fine . . . Carlson's writing is crisp and blunt, much like the very Wyoming landscape he describes. *The Signal* is about small, tight things that widen out into immensities. It is about love and regret and the pain of loss and the wild parts of Wyoming."
—Julia Keller, *Chicago Tribune*

"Ron Carlson's the kind of writer who's easy to underestimate. His short fiction is consistently excellent, and his casual, unpretentious style is reinforced by his reputation as a teacher. . . . At its core [*The Signal*] is a story about a troubled man trying to work his way back to true north."
—*The Oregonian* (Portland)

"There's more intense action crammed into Ron Carlson's brief new novel than in many works twice its length. Couple that with two complex and absorbing protagonists and gorgeous writing that pays homage to the natural world, and you have a deeply appealing work that's easy to appreciate on a variety of levels. No doubt some readers will hear echoes of Ernest Hemingway or Cormac McCarthy in *The Signal*'s clean, tightly controlled prose and its story of the small scale of human travails when played out against the gorgeous but unforgiving natural world. Yet it would be a disservice to Ron Carlson to suggest that this accomplished work is in any way derivative of these masters. In truth, he has created something equally masterful of his own."

—Bookreporter.com

"Carlson describes the couple's six days wandering the wooded terrain in delicate, measured prose, careful to miss neither the lush scenery nor the incrementally amplified tension as Mack edges closer to his prize and shady characters from Mack's past appear. Carlson has produced a work of masterful fiction, combining the sad inevitability of a doomed relationship with sheer nail-biting suspense."

—*Publishers Weekly* (starred review)

"Energetic description of rocky mountain romance . . . the novel simmers with a strongly constructed impression of trouble perpetually lurking nearby."

—*Kirkus Reviews*

"As in his finely wrought *Five Skies*, Carlson excels in painting a stunningly beautiful portrait of a place. . . . Vivid . . . There is plenty to enjoy here, from the portrayal of the majestic mountains to the interplay between the lead characters."

—*Booklist*

ABOUT THE AUTHOR

Ron Carlson is the author of four story collections and four novels, most recently *Five Skies*. His fiction has appeared in *Harper's*, *The New Yorker*, *Playboy*, and *GQ*. His work has been featured in NPR's *This American Life* and *Selected Shorts* and in *Best American Short Stories* and *The O. Henry Prize Stories*. He is the directory of the UC Irvine writing program and lives in Huntington Beach, California.

THE SIGNAL

RON CARLSON

PENGUIN BOOKS

For Elaine

This is a work of fiction. No events or persons are real. Some of the place names, mountains, and fish are real, but I have moved them around in writing the story. Also I've made the fish a little bigger than they actually are. This is hope at work, an elemental feature of storytelling.

I wish to thank Roger Day who showed me his marked copy of Finis Mitchell's fine book, *Wind River Trails*, and then the mountains themselves. A note: if I was going to go into the Wind Rivers today, I would use the Bears Ears trailhead and I would go before September 10.

I wrote this book in October at Ucross and I am grateful to the Ucross Foundation, especially Sharon Dynak and all of the staff. My thanks also to my friend Michelle Latiolais.

PENGUIN BOOKS

Published by the Penguin Group
Penguin Group (USA) Inc., 375 Hudson Street, New York, New York 10014, U.S.A.
Penguin Group (Canada), 90 Eglinton Avenue East, Suite 700, Toronto, Ontario, Canada M4P 2Y3 (a division of Pearson Penguin Canada Inc.) • Penguin Books Ltd, 80 Strand, London WC2R 0RL, England • Penguin Ireland, 25 St Stephen's Green, Dublin 2, Ireland (a division of Penguin Books Ltd) • Penguin Group (Australia), 250 Camberwell Road, Camberwell, Victoria 3124, Australia (a division of Pearson Australia Group Pty Ltd) • Penguin Books India Pvt Ltd, 11 Community Centre, Panchsheel Park, New Delhi – 110 017, India • Penguin Group (NZ), 67 Apollo Drive, Rosedale, North Shore 0632, New Zealand (a division of Pearson New Zealand Ltd) • Penguin Books (South Africa) (Pty) Ltd, 24 Sturdee Avenue, Rosebank, Johannesburg 2196, South Africa

Penguin Books Ltd, Registered Offices: 80 Strand, London WC2R 0RL, England

First published in the United States of America by Viking Penguin,
a member of Penguin Group (USA) Inc. 2009
Published in Penguin Books 2010

10 9 8 7 6 5 4 3 2 1

THE LIBRARY OF CONGRESS HAS CATALOGED THE HARDCOVER EDITION AS FOLLOWS:
Carlson, Ron.
The signal : a novel / Ron Carlson.
p.   cm.
ISBN 978-0-670-02100-0 (hc.)
ISBN 978-0-14-311755-1 (pbk.)
1. Title.
PS35553.A733S54 2009
813'.54—dc22   2008046690

Printed in the United States of America
Set in Aldus • Designed by Alissa Amell

Day One

He drove the smooth winding two-track up through the high aspen grove and crossed the open meadow to the edge of the pines at the Cold Creek trailhead and parked his father's old blue Chevrolet pickup by the ruined sign in the September twilight. He had been right: there were no other vehicles. There had been no fresh tire tracks on the ten-mile ascent from the old highway except for the set of duals that had come almost halfway and turned around. That would have been Bluebride's horse trailer seeing to his cattle the week before. Mack had seen two dozen head scattered in the low sage all along the way. He got out of the truck and reached back for the coffee he'd picked up at the Crowheart general store an hour ago; it was cold. He walked back and opened the tailgate and sat, finally lifting his eyes to look east across the tiers of Wyoming spread beneath him in the vast echelons of brown and gray. It was dark here against the forest, but light gathered across the planet and he could see the golden horizon at a hundred and fifty miles. He wanted to see headlights, but there were none. He wanted to see headlights bumping up the old road to meet him here, at the appointed hour.

He could tell that it had already snowed once, sometime last week, but there was no sign of it now, no patches in the deep shade, no mud in the tracks, but the country was blonder, the grasses still standing but bleached once, paler, as if slapped by the first weather of the season. Mack sipped the cold coffee thick with cream and looked for her car. She would come or she wouldn't come, and he would still have his mission. He said it aloud. "She'll come or she won't, but you're still going in."

He stood down and retrieved the brown fleece vest she'd given him five years ago, and he moved to the toolbox and got out his stove and set it up on the tailgate and filled his old pan half full of water and put it on the blue ring of flame. He pulled his pack off the front seat and knelt in the grass against the wall of trees and set up his old two-man, a blue and gray throwback twenty years old; he'd replaced many of the wands twice, but the zippers still worked. He threw his pad and sleeping bag into the tent and then laid the little raggy carpet sample on the ground at the entry. He'd been barefoot on it a hundred times in the mountains. Some things you carried in because they made sense. It was dark working there, but again behind the truck the light of the world fell on his shoulders. To the north he could see one corner of the highway so far below and those cars now had their lights on. He checked his pack for the electronics that Yarnell had given him: the military BlackBerry; he had it in foil in a small Velveeta box. He double-checked all his side pockets and then he unrolled his fishing vest and checked the nine pockets in it for all his fishing gear. He repacked and clipped his rod segments along the back, and then laid it all on the front seat. He was ready.

He took his bonus cooler, the old green metal Coleman from their dating days and knelt and pushed it under the truck behind the cab. They always did it, left a cooler full of goodies for the day out. He could hear the water roiling on his stove now and he walked back there and put in a finger loop of angel hair and then another. If she doesn't come, I'll eat double and sleep like a bear. He walked off and pissed in the open meadow and lit one of his cheap wood-tipped cigarillos with his father's lighter, a Zippo that had been around the world twice in the old man's pocket on troopships. Mack was not scared. He had been uneasy and worried and scared and empty and sort of ruined, and he knew this, but now he had his ways of doing one thing and then the next and it kept the ruin off him. If she left Jackson by four, she'd be along in a while. If she hadn't left Jackson; well then.

She'd come down to the county jail a month ago where there wasn't a visiting room, and Zeff Minatas had brought him out to the coffee room and let them talk for twenty minutes. He could not look at her and after a full minute she said softly, "Well."

It took him three attempts to break through the whisper and say, "You bet. Now I'm in the ashes." Each tear cost him, but he could not with his breath prevent them. He hadn't been in a room with her all year and now the quiet in his heart burned again.

"You're going to climb out of this."

"Somehow," he said. He was talking straight down, to the table.

"You look rough," she said. "You lost some weight."

"Yeah, well. I'm about broke down actually." That was all he could master and he sat still.

Zeff came in and set out two Styrofoam cups and filled each from his own Stanley thermos, steaming coffee. "There's cream already in there," he pointed.

When he capped the thermos and stepped out, Vonnie said, "Am I worried?"

Her voice cracked him, every word. He could shake his head and he did.

"Yes," she said. "I am. Look, Mack. You'll be all right. Things will get better."

"Disgrace," he said.

"What?"

"I am a disgrace," he said.

Now she read him accurately. "You been this low?"

He could not speak.

"When you get out Wednesday, can you get yourself together? What do you need for gear? Do you have a ride?"

Her solicitous questions broke over him. He could hold steady against his own withering self-regard, but he could not hold against her sympathy. When she put her hand on his wrist, the shock ran through him.

"Chester will come get me."

"He's a good friend," she said. "Go fishing for a week. This will pass."

"No can do."

Then she leaned toward him and spoke against the top of his head. "Mack, don't let this beat you. You're a good man inside."

Now the tears tripled dripping onto the shirtsleeve of his jail shirt.

She pushed his coffee until the cup touched his interleaved hands. "Here," she said, "drink this. Remember your coffee policy." It was an old bit of theirs, but he could not respond.

"Meet me," she said. "You can do that, right? We'll make our last trip next month. Meet me, and we'll fish Clark Lake for the last time."

Somehow air came into his chest with that and he said quietly, "Deal." He looked up into her face, the seriousness and the concern. He opened his hand and closed it around the little white cup. "I will be there. Cold Creek trailhead."

He'd been here ten times; this was the tenth time. Every year on the same day, the Ides of September, nine fifteen. The promise had been made that first time and they'd kept it nine times. *We'll do this every year.* They weren't married the first time, and then they had been married eight times, and now they weren't married again. As far as he knew. The lawyer letters, five of them, were filed unopened in a cubby of his father's rolltop in the bunkhouse where Mack lived on the home place south of Woodrow, golden envelopes with return addresses pretty as wedding invitations.

He felt better tonight, strong for some reason, but he'd been getting better since walking out of jail twenty days ago. It could have been so much worse. He'd been running in low-rent behavior for almost a year, scrambling for money, crossing the line when it worked for him, drinking too much because it didn't matter and the company he kept drank. He had trouble with the mortgage at the ranch, and he'd driven cars to Cheyenne and Rock Springs more than once not asking what was in the trunk, just taking the thousand bucks and walking away. He'd been an idiot and he'd rusted like an old post when the weather turned. Now he shook his head at it in dark wonder. It was like the old song. He once was lost and now he was found, though there wasn't much left. He knew this trip was the right thing and he'd even gotten well enough to call her and let her off the hook. Last week he'd left a message saying it was okay if she couldn't make it and that he appreciated the help. He knew where there were some fish. He

didn't want the sympathy vote, didn't need it, but, he told her, he
was going fishing at the appointed hour.

He'd met Vonnie when they were both seventeen, and he
didn't like her immediately, because it was his personal policy to
dislike all the people who came to the ranch, the families from
Grosse Pointe and Greenwich and Manhattan and Princeton and
from the ten other platinum republics in their beautiful flannel
shirts and new Levi's. He treated them well and saw to their safety
around the horses, and he taught them what he could about the
ranch and securing knots and fire safety and the birds and the
snakes and the occasional bears. He took them to Big Springs and
Rocktree trailheads, but he didn't bring them here. He envied
their gear, their bright boots, their gorgeous bone pocketknives,
but he never stole one. He was quiet and known as being quiet
and it was not an act; he had learned that it was the way he kept
any power at all. After his mother died of the cancer and his father and the ranch manager, Sawyer Day, saw the money story,
they had started taking ten weeks of guests in the summers. They
needed the money. They hired a great cook, a woman named Amarantha out of Logan, Utah, and she laid a table like he had never
seen. For that time the ranch paid its bills. The reputation of Box
Creek grew, and they were booked steady all those years: twenty-
four people every week, and Mack grew up with them from when
he was ten, answering the same questions about horseshoes and
hay and can I feed this horse an apple without him biting me. A
horse on a dude ranch eats a lot of apples. Vonnie's family came
out from Chapel Hill where her mother was a professor of political science, and he gave her the same horse every year, Rusty, a

benevolent roan who was golden once a day if the sun was right. Vonnie was a strong athlete and played soccer in college, but Mack avoided her (as he did all the guests) easily. Many weeks the guests had romances with the other guests, intrigues afoot, and Mack had plenty of work grooming horses when the day ended while everyone showered in the big house and in the two cottages and then lined up for Amarantha's astounding buffet.

Plus, his father had spoken to him after the third summer. It was obvious the way the kids hung out by the rail fence when Mack was shoeing a horse or working the tack. They'd follow him around, the boys and the girls, and they wanted to know about him.

His father called him into the big house and they sat in the small front office that Sawyer Day used the two days a week he came out to do books, and his father swiveled the oak chair to Mack and they talked. The room was cloistered by the varnished pine shelves full of books, his father's collection of Zane Grey and Jack London and western history and a beaten tin umbrella stand full of rolled maps.

"These kids look up to you," his father said.

"I don't know," Mack said. He sat on the dark leather hassock, orphaned from its long-lost chair.

"Yes you do. They should look up to you. You're a good hand; they're not used to this. All they've got is their car and the junior prom. You're an exotic item, Mack."

"Okay," the boy said.

"But what we are to these people is a sort of cliché. They come out here to taste this and it's good for all of us. But these girls,

some of them, are going to fall for you, you big strong cowboy."
His father tapped Mack's knee with his two fingers. "Come on,
you can look at me. I know you're a good kid. Some of these gals
from New York even come after your old man, a little fling out
west for a week. You want to be a cliché?"

"No sir," Mack said. "I don't."

"You need me to recount the history of Sheridan the race-
horse?"

"No sir, please."

His father smiled. "Have you recovered from that lesson?"
He'd taken the boy to witness their only Thoroughbred, Sheridan, at stud when Mack was nine years old.

"No sir," Mack said truly. "No one could." Mack went on and
repeated what his father had said that day, "That's enough of the
birds and bees for one boy."

"Well, good," his father said. "We won't be clichés then. That's
all. I expect you know what to do. Talk the day with these kids and
riding and horses and weather, and then send them back to supper.
Don't walk with them or have them out near the bunkhouse. My
eyes are right here. I know you know what to do. I don't want this
business venture we're in to hurt you, boy. I love you and I love
this place. Do you know it?"

"Yes sir, I do."

"Show me your hands." Mack leaned and held his hands out
and then turned them over. They'd always done this: a show of
hands. His father looked him over: nails, cuticles, knuckles, palms.
You could tell a good ranch hand by the number of nicks—the
fewer, the better the ranch hand, and as the years passed, Mack's

hands cleared up. His father squeezed his hands now and said, "That's enough of that. Quite a talk for the old homestead. You go, get to work."

And he did the work on the long day ranch schedule. On Thursday nights he ran the one late-night campfire, all those chocolate crackers and then the spooky story. He had started it when he was thirteen, the story he'd heard part of from his own dad about Hiram, brokenhearted and half mad, who still roamed the woods near here, living in rotten logs and following campers in his search for a beating heart. At night when the fishermen's campfires would shrink down to wavering coals, Hiram would sneak into the camps and reach into the tents and put his head against the campers' chests to try to hear again the thumping of a heart. His own had stopped so long ago. Mack would let the big ranch fire dwindle and collapse and lower his voice as he told the episodes. Hiram's heart had been broken by his own true love when one night he came calling and saw her through the lighted window in the arms of another man.

"A fisherman?" some kid would ask.

"Not much of one," Mack would say, "but maybe. And Hiram turned and fled that place and went into the woods, these woods, forever."

Half of the kids would already be in their pajamas and robes, sitting legs up and arms folded in the canvas camp chairs, listening. They'd all heard of Hiram from last week or from last summer, and his legend was part of the Box Creek Ranch lore now. Mack would hold out his hand like a claw and say how Hiram only wanted human contact. "His loneliness was larger than

Wyoming. He only wanted then to hear a beating heart. But he was misunderstood and called a cannibal, though there was never any proof of that."

"I think he was a cannibal," some boy would say. "He ate the campers and cooked them over the fire. They never came back."

Mack would let this remark hang in the air. "He's out there," Mack would say, indicating the circle of darkness around them all. "And now we know for sure he's misunderstood."

If the children got too frightened, which was why they came every week, Mack would back up and tell about Hiram's younger days working with wild geese and his travels in the cities which did not agree with him. Then as the hour turned, Mack would stand and stir the fire pit and as the cinders schooled up red, he would say, "Hiram listens for a beating heart. Can you hear your beating heart?" The night would glow with silence and the popping of the fire. "Now scoot. We're going to ride horses tomorrow, and I don't want you falling asleep."

It was a favorite time for him, watching the young people scurry back to the cabins' lit porches. They tried not to run, but they sometimes ran. It was his first love, the ranch, and he loved it night and day.

Then came his second.

The year he was seventeen, Mack took the weekly ridge ride with all the kids, nine riders winding up the line shack trail to the aspen draws that led to the mountaintop. He rode his horse Copper Bob, the captain. There were two old log cabins along the way, slumped and fallen in, new trees thrusting through the collapsed roof beams. They always stopped and took stagey pictures with the young people pretending to knock at the doorway or looking out the ancient window frames. Sometimes they dug around for old cans or bottles, and they made up stories about the lonely men who lived here, how they had a dog or played cards all winter. One of the young riders would always say, Maybe this is where Hiram lived, and Mack would explain that he never slept in the same place twice. He was always wandering and without a home.

The cabins always sobered Mack, because he knew how hard such lives would have been. Over the years he'd found and kept purple medicine bottles and boot buckles from the old places. Vonnie was a good rider and Rusty knew her, and they liked to lead the train through the gloomy treeshade. The horses stepped quietly up the grassy slopes, past the wildflowers, along the faint trail they'd walked a hundred times, their tails swishing silently timed to the gait. Mack watched the girl float in her saddle at the top of the easy parade. This was the golden center of Mack's life, all these fine animals geared right and taking the bobbing children up every step farther from home than they had ever been.

Mack saw a shadow in the hillside and knew what it was in a second; he sat up and snugged his reins from where he rode behind the children. When the bear sat up in the tall June grass at the top of the draw, Mack thought he saw him rub his eyes like a man might in disbelief. It was a luxurious black bear and he didn't stand or look alarmed. He sat and looked into the face of the first horse. Mack had known moments like this and usually something happened very fast as the surprises doubled. Rusty stopped short without rearing, but Vonnie went over the front of her saddle and fell. Mack felt something open in him. All the horses stopped, veterans. Mack knew that when Rusty turned riderless, all the horses would turn and start stepping down. He loved it that they knew not to run. They never ran even on the last flat stretch near the ranch yard, even when the tourists urged them with their heels or reins or any cowboy moves they had seen in films for years on end.

Mack was moving; he clucked and Copper Bob eyed the bear and still approached. Vonnie was down and Mack had to get down and lift her with an arm and lead the horse to turn away. The bear hadn't moved, watching the performance. At twenty paces Mack boosted the girl up into his saddle and walked surely down behind the children's cavalcade which was now headed inexorably toward the ranch, two miles below. Those who had been at the rear and hadn't seen the bear would be astonished and envious as they heard the story, but by supper they would have their own tales of the close call and the huge beast. As they passed below the cabin shambles and onto the open hillside, Mack whistled and Rusty stopped and the line of riders stopped.

"Are you okay?" Mack said.

"It was a bear," Vonnie said. She was lit. They reached her horse and Mack helped her down.

"Let's see." She had skinned her wrist, and she pulled out her shirt and showed him where her waist was bruised, her belt full of dirt and grass.

"I'm okay. Can we go back and get a picture?" Everybody had a camera.

"Not today," he said. "That bear doesn't want his picture taken today." He still had her arm and turned her in examination.

"Did he attack?" one of the kids said.

"No," Mack said. "He was sleeping and we woke him up."

"Hibernating," one of the kids said.

"Not yet," Mack said. "Let's go down." He held Rusty while Vonnie mounted. She was turned looking back up at the hill.

"That bear was hibernating. Bears hibernate," the expert offered again.

"Go go," Mack called and the line of horses and riders began the walk home.

It was the next morning that Mack had a problem. He woke to a face in his window: Copper Bob, and he pulled on his Levi's and boots and stepped onto the porch to find the dozen ranch horses all standing in the bunkhouse dooryard. Above, he could see the corral gate open. With his boots unlaced and his shirt unbuttoned, he walked up there clucking for Copper Bob who led the others back into the enclosure. By the time he closed the rail gate, Mack knew that Rusty was gone. He saddled Copper Bob and rode over to the main house. Amarantha was in the kitchen and the whole place smelled like batter, her blueberry pancakes.

"Can you do the Dutch oven today?" he asked her. "I've got to go find a horse."

"We can do that, Mack." She had six cast-iron ovens and cooked with the young people a day or two every week over the fire pit behind the house.

"Save me some pancakes," he said.

He knew what it was and trotted Copper Bob up the ranching road and into the trees, past the cabins. The dew was disturbed all the way, and he slowed in the aspen draw and saw where she had ridden up through and over the top. A bear chaser.

Above, he came out of the trees and ascended the ridgeline.

There was a game trail that traced the spine of the broad hill and led to the mountains ahead. "Goddamnit," he said and followed it up. He could see Rusty's shoeprints in the clay trail periodically and horse manure as the trail dipped and rose again now into the pines. He was also looking for bear sign and there was none.

In the old days this was where the first ranchers had baited bear with horse carcasses, walking an old horse up to the top and then shooting it right at the wall of trees, someplace they could watch from across the canyon. Eighty years ago these pioneers had picnicked and waited with their rifles. There were still old constellations of horse skeletons drifting down a slope here and there. All the way to the horizon west and south was federal land and always had been, open to hunting in season. At the end of every summer Mack took four or five of the experienced riders out through the federal land and into the national forest, dead-heading sometimes, learning the country. He liked being out be-yond what he knew. Every year they came across butchered elk, chainsawed by poachers, the head and hindquarters taken months before the season. He hated these things, and he banked his ha-tred for such characters. He marked their trails when he could, but nothing came of his research.

One year his father had gone off two days with four rangers and the civil patrol raiding a poacher's camp, and when his father returned, he unloaded his horse from the trailer and put away the tack without speaking. Mack wanted to know what had happened, but his father's face told him not to ask. He later found out one of the men, a teamster from Hammond, had tried for his rifle and been shot dead.

Now Mack was in the pines, the trail narrow at points and

moist, and still he saw where Rusty had tracked. He spent an hour like that in and out of the trees, breaking into the sage day, the hundred-mile vistas and then again into the green dark. "God-damn girl," he said. At the saddle near the summit, he stopped and whistled three times, the way he could, the sharpest loudest noise a human can make. Nothing. A little ahead he saw where Rusty had left the trail and begun to descend the far slope. Oh shit shit shit. It was noon, the day was gone. He should have brought the walkie-talkies, his rifle, a lunch. "Girl," he called. "Rusty," he called. She was off the trail now, sidehilling the sage to who knew where. The way was steep and there were shale outcroppings. At least it was clear and sunny, but the day was gone. They'd never lost a girl before. They'd had blisters and splinters and hangovers and one broken arm when a boy fell off the corral fence, but no one had been lost. No one had perished. On the shady side of the mountain fourteen bighorn sheep ascended in bursts up the sandy mountainside, tame as barngoats, and obliterated the girl's trail. He rode out looking for the tracks and could not find them. She either went up or down and now it was three o'clock. To hell with you. Mack knew that Rusty would know when the sun hit four to head for home. If she was still aboard. To hell with you and your camera, lady. This far from the ranch there were three or four ways back, and Mack climbed up and over the summit and then just guessed the stream trail and struck for that, a mile and a half east. It was warm in the sun and fresh in the shadows, climbing down. He was deadheading it, but he had been gifted with direc-tional skill that even his father remarked on. He hit the Box Creek and watered Copper Bob and then led him by the reins up to the log bridge he had built with his father ten years before, when he was seven. His father taught him the chainsaw and let him run it, bucking the thin logs into five-foot lengths for the flooring. All that green wood was now dried slate gray and appeared an artifact of the frontier.

Before he saw the bridge, he heard Copper Bob snuffle and there was Rusty tied to a tree. The girl was lying on the bridge, her arms out as if she had fallen from a great height. She was bare-legged and her new brown corduroy jeans lay jumbled by her head. Mack and Copper Bob walked up.

"You asleep?"

She looked at him without moving her head, her face upside down to him. "I'm okay." She pulled her shirttail down over her underwear. "I guess I'm lost," she said.

He stood silent; the two horses nosed each other. Mack held the horse. He could see the angry red chafe on her thighs.

"What's your name again?" she said.

"I guess your bear got away." He stepped up and checked Rusty's saddle which was secure and the bridle. "You did a good job with this gear."

"I can't ride anymore," she said. "I can't touch my legs."

"We just need to get back and then you can soak," he told her. "We have to go though."

She sat up and looked at her inflamed legs. She stood and pulled her pants on, tenderly. "Oh god, I can't even walk."

"You're about skinned," he said, "but I've seen worse. Move through it," he said. "We'll get you to the ranch road and I can bring the truck."

"How far is that?"

"Up over there and down: two miles, a little more."

She stepped stiffly to the horse and Mack helped her up. She moaned and said, "Where's that bear?"

"Montana," he told her. "You scared that bear a good one jumping on him that way."

She laughed and cried out softly as Rusty followed Copper Bob across the old wooden bridge and into the glade. "What's your name," she had said.

In the glowing mountain dark Mack walked across the dirt path of the trailhead to the old Forest Service sign hanging now by one rusty bolt. The post was still grounded firmly. He went back to his toolbox in the truck and retrieved the two six-inch steel bolts and the nuts and wide lock washers as well as his closed wrench and hacksaw. The old bolt fell away with five strokes of the saw and the sign dropped. Mack held it in both hands. The paint in the routed letters was all gone, and he had actually thought of bringing paint, but it would have been overdoing it and bright lettering always invited vandalism. He fitted it up and placed it square and took pleasure in cinching the nuts on tight as they bit into the old stained pine. *Cold Creek Trailhead.* The first time he'd come here, his father had sent him across to the sign and there was a small plastic envelope wedged behind, between the sign and the post. He withdrew it and found a dollar bill and a Royal Coachman fly and a small card that said, "Let's fish, Mack. Love, Dad." He still had the scrap in his wallet. Now he folded the baggie he'd brought and hid it in the back, against the old splintered post, securing it with a silver pushpin. If she comes, she'll surely check the mail.

He went back across and put his tools away and opened the

hood and checked the oil. It was dark there, and he used his flash-light. Small actions kept the worry off. If he hadn't just done it, he would have tucked his shirt in again. He washed his hands. Oh September, you beauty. Show me something.

That winter after he'd shown her the bears, she wrote him one letter from Brown that told him her family was coming the second week in August. They had wanted to go to Martha's Vineyard, but she had held out. She told them she had an appointment with a bear and signed it: *Vonnie, Music Major, Bearhunter.*

He spent July scouting the western hills and found them one at a time: six black bears, two cubs, one still cinnamon. The next month when her family arrived, he stayed busy, and the two young people ignored each other. There was a lot to do. The third day at dawn, the day Amarantha was going to get out the Dutch ovens and make biscuits and omelettes with the kids, he came to the porch rail of the bunkhouse and he could see the girl on the porch of her little cottage. She stood and followed him to the corral. They rode two hours out the trail he had marked until they were in a hollow above the valley of the bears. They hadn't spoken.

"How are your legs?"

"Good," she said. "You've seen worse."

"You bring your camera?" he asked her.

"I've got it."

"Do you want to see these bears?"

"Yes, I do. I came to see a bear, one will do."

"I'm not sure I should let you at them," he said.

"And why is that?"

"Because once you get your bear, you'll be done with me."

She turned in her saddle, one hand on the back of it, and said, "I haven't even started with you."

"You don't know my name."

"I know your name."

"Don't say it."

"Don't you say my name."

Mack said: "Do you keep your word?"

"Yes, mister, I do."

"Come along then." He led her up through the trees to the overlook. Below, the vale was meadow and aspen that gave way to the pines. They wended down a rocky trail, staying above the open area. They sat and the horses knew to be still.

This was his life, riding out two hours from a ranch that itself was an hour from town and still knowing there were unknown hours ahead. The ridges of the next valley were distinct and thrilling in the clear summer air. He'd been there once or twice maybe; he remembered a swale with two reedy moose pots against a granite hill, but it was trackless and like so much up here, it was still waiting. Someone had told him that there were only a few places left in the country where a person could get five miles from the road, and it remained the worst news he'd ever heard. He wasn't himself in town, and though he liked school, the energy, and could bear a semester, he didn't really trust that world, or himself in it, and at the end of every term his car was packed before the last exam and then he fled home, fled to the hills. Two hawks swung out into the blue-sky sunshine and traded treetops in the valley below them.

"Music?" he said.

"There's no money in it, but I'm a music major."

"You play the piano?"

"That and the clarinet." She scanned the treetops and the meadow greenery below and said, "They're close, aren't they?"

"They are," he said. "It's about bear time." Then he added, "I can't even play a guitar."

"That's good. You'd be the whole package as a cowboy who played guitar."

A black bear on all fours walked out into the sunlight.

"Is it the same bear?" she whispered. A smaller bear appeared at the edge of the trees.

"They're all the same bear."

She lifted her lensed Nikon out of its case and began to take pictures. As the camera sneezed, the bears lifted their heads to look up. "Yes, it's him, my same bear." She turned and took Mack's picture. When she had packed her camera away and lifted it behind her back, she said to him, "Thanks for this." He reined Copper Bob around on the narrow trail and started back.

His father came out to the tack room that afternoon and stood in the sunlit doorway. "You're doing something?"

"Yes, sir, I am. Not much, but I am."

"Do you know what you're doing?"

"No, sir, I don't."

"Are you going by your gut?"

"By something."

"Do you think you can get a girl by showing her a bear?"

"No idea," Mack said.

His father folded his arms and leaned on the doorframe. "Me neither. How many were there?"

"Seven or eight. Three cubs."

"There's good news."

Mack waited. He knew his father had something else. "I showed your mother two hundred elk in an aspen grove high above the reservoir at Cody."

"Sir?"

"And two years later I was a married man."

"Who got whom?" Mack said, a gambit.

"We're still not sure," his father said. "Just that it was a good deal." He stood and held his hands out lightly at his waist. "A girl who goes for a bear is superior to one who would go for a car. I'll say that. You just be careful of yourself. Remember Jude?" Jude had been their first hand, a drunk, always cutting himself or losing things with bad knots. He finally fell from a horse and put an eye out on a fence post.

"I'll be careful," Mack said.

"Oh, I know it," his father said. "You're not the least like Jude, but your old man wants to worry. You know?" His father stepped and put his hand on the boy's neck and embraced him just a moment.

"Don't I know it," Mack said to the man. Then he stood and faced his father. "This isn't a cliché and it won't be. It's either nothing or something, but don't worry."

The next January he got the pictures, the bears, and himself on Copper Bob, his face half shaded by his hat. The letter said she'd be in Europe all the next summer and for him not to show those bears to any other person. He was at Boise State studying history and everything else, lots of computer stuff. He liked everything but accounting.

Without her, the ranch that summer was different and he used the energy he felt when she was around to work at learning the money of it, their never-ending hard stretch. Sawyer Day and his father sold sections; there was pressure for houses, mansions really, and with each sale they bought a year or two, but the taxes and the mortgage were still significant. He applied to have the tax status changed to ranching and the county changed it to modified-use estate range residential. They had some terms. He applied again. With his father in trouble like that it was hard to concentrate on his studies the next fall, but they advanced, and he pursued computer science, encryption as it developed, and modern history.

Then two things happened in one day the next winter. He'd taken a house across downtown, a gerrymandered brick bungalow where he lived alone and had his computers lined up serially in the front room. He wanted a set of components and objectives he could control. He was consulting for the university and on a State Department grant. There were two phone calls in one day. One was the girl calling from Prague. She would finish her degree in May and was coming west.

She said, "This is a job interview: I want to work at the Box Creek and buy that horse. And I need to tell you a secret." The long-distance line was a steady friction.

"I can't stop you," he said.

Then he heard her whisper: "I said your name."

His heart clogged his throat. A minute later he said, "Come west. Bring your diploma and get out here."

Before he had sat on the ratty couch he'd covered with a bedsheet, Sawyer Day called and asked him if he was sitting down.

His father's death changed it all. At the ranch everything was tilted, weird; it was more than something missing. Gravity had changed. Mack saw to the horses and painted the small barn, but there was no center for him without his father there. He made an effort to focus and failed; he felt there was no reason to brush the horses, no reason to feed himself. His grief was tangled by the enormity of the place and the fact that he felt he didn't deserve it. When he came into the house, the feeling of emptiness rocked him. He hadn't seen his father every day, but he knew his father was there, out at the ranch or in the other room or coming back from town and his presence in the world was like order itself. It was impossible to fathom and for the whole season he had trouble pushing one foot in front of another, trouble tying his work boots in the first place. Some rule had been expunged and he felt off-step and wrongheaded. The daylight of the dear place had changed.

And not just the ranch; when he was back at school Boise felt like it was underwater. He stopped going to class and started cutting corners with his computer work. His life, which had seemed a logical series of clear choices, blurred for a moment and then blurred for real. Without his father's expectations, he found himself without a rudder and he knew it, and he drew a sharp breath when he saw that there was some part of him that was glad for it.

Mack's father was buried in the family yard atop the northern hill beside Mack's mother. The black wrought-iron fence had been welded in the toolshed below. Years ago Mack's mother had planted the dozen golden juniper pfitzers that struggled in the wind but survived. Sawyer helped Mack. They closed the guest ranch and battened down the hatches. Sawyer showed him all the numbers; they were negative always six hundred and fifty dollars a month. They sold acreage so they had two years. Sawyer waived his fee and stepped away, shaking Mack's hand. "I hope you can keep the place."

There were still 375 acres of range and hill and mountain, down from over a thousand fifty years before. He had twenty offers on the place, enough to retire on. He sold the two cute log cabin cottages and they were hauled off on flatbeds. He sold all the horses but three. Amarantha drove out from town one day and gave him a notebook with her recipes and kissed him on the cheeks. The printing was beautiful and large, but he knew he'd never make a one. He wired up his computers and went from grant to grant, now working in codes for this agency and then that. People in town thought him a hermit. He was twenty years old.

In June a black Range Rover pulled into the ranch dooryard and a man that Mack recognized got out. His name was Charley Yarnell, and he'd been a guest several summers at the ranch.

"I liked your father," he told Mack, "and I wanted to talk to you."

"The place is not for sale," Mack said. "We're flush."

"You're not flush," Charley said, "but I don't care. I want you to do some work for us. From out here. Consulting." They sat in the front parlor, a room dominated by his mother's bright rag rug, an oval of orange and red and blue and green that looked like the bottom of a trout stream. "This is good work," Charley said.

"Money, and somebody's got to do it. You'd be an outpost, like a transfer station."

"This country is full of retired military," Mack told him. "People with clearance."

"That right there says it all. I don't need people with clearance. I need somebody at the end of the road."

"Is it the CIA?" Mack asked.

"Nothing is the CIA," Charley said. "It's just an agency and it's just a job. The only people who would talk about it would be you and me."

"This is a favor?" Mack asked him.

"No, it's work. I saw you with your dad; you're my man."

"I'm not my dad," Mack said. It hurt to say and was a relief. "You want some tea?"

"No," Charley said. "I want you to put in a satellite dish for TV, any company you want, and I want to give you this card." There was a twelve-digit number on the card. Charley stood, and the two men shook hands. "This is good for you," Charley said. "I'm sure of that. But hear me: this is good for me. I'll be talking to you."

When Yarnell drove out of the ranch yard, Mack felt doubt sweep over like cover. He knew the man was marginal. His father had said something, but he couldn't remember it. He did recall the way his father dealt with slippery characters, and he called them slippery, many times CEOs at the ranch who would rather talk business than go hiking, asking about the numbers and lifestyle. His father always put on his old world manners with such people, the rectitude, politeness, and posture. Mack could read it from across the yard, watching his father keeping every moment square and measured as if reading from the big book. "Manners are not frosting on the cake, Mack," his father had told him. "Manners, chapter and verse, are protection. They can be better than muscle in the slippery places. A strong man is strong enough to hold himself back." The other part he taught him very young was that "a man can do more at a rough or tricky dinner with a napkin than he can with a fork."

Mack began relaying coded pages two or three times a month, and the checks, enough to keep him afloat, arrived by courier every month as well. He could tell from the formats that half the stuff was going to embassies and military bases. He didn't care. He banked the money and wondered if he was doing the right thing for a few minutes every week; what was it when you could do something well, but you didn't know what you were doing? He just went on automatic pilot and looked the other way. It wasn't his father's way, but his father was gone.

The girl was out there somewhere, and he steeled his heart to the fact that she'd met someone and he'd get a clipping from one of the papers with her wedding announcement. He'd been busy and worried, but it hadn't masked the other thing, a feeling he had for her.

She called in September from a school outside of Minneapolis where she was teaching music theory. "Who's calling?" he said.

"You don't know my name," she said, "but we've met."

"Give me your address," he said, "I've got a proposal for you."

"Careful with your language."

"I'm careful with everything."

He then sent her a hand-drawn map on the back of a paper

placemat that indicated the Crowheart general store and how many miles it was to the unmarked turnoff to the trailhead and then a dotted line up the dirt road to the Cold Creek trailhead where he drew an X and noted: September 15. 5:00 P.M.

A month later he stood where he was tonight under earth's sky as the twilight thickened in gradations across the vastness. That first night he had brought all the gear for both of them, and when her old Volvo bounced up into the trailhead flat, he knew what he knew. That was ten years ago.

Tonight it was now the grainy dark of dreams, and he stirred the pasta, slicing in the Italian sausage from Hershmeyer's in Jackson. Homemade sausage. He set out the straw-bound bottle of Chianti. Dinner for one. He'd open the wine for her if she came. His own drinking days were over and he knew it. You make yourself sick enough, you don't go back. He had his father's spine in the matter. He was on the other side of it now, and he didn't know what the days would bring him except none of that. The Wind River Range lay behind him in the new night, a place he loved and would never know fully from all the years behind and all the years ahead. No one could take it. Now he could feel the altitude in his heartbeat.

Then there was a sound like a river rock walking down a stream bottom, a muted concussion that slowly grew and became the sound of a car working up the dirt trail road. It was a silver Lexus with the lights out in the gloaming and it came across the space and eased in next to his truck. The tinted window went down and there was her face.

"Hey, mister," she said. "This road is full of cattle tonight."

He found his voice. "Those are Bluebride's. He hasn't gotten them down yet. How have you been?" he asked her. "Nice car."

"Yeah, well."

"Kent got it for you?"

"He helped. It belongs to the school."

"He gave it to the school."

She got out. "What are you cooking, the pasta?"

"Yes, ma'am, as always."

Vonnie rubbed her face and took it all in. Each minute now the darkness doubled in the mountain night. "Oh, this place."

"Ten years," he said.

"Ten years," she said. "The last trip."

"You came," he said. He forked the pasta up in a test. "You kept your word."

She looked at him, "Mack," she said. "It's been a hideous year and you hideous in it, but it's my word."

Day Two

In the morning they walked in. The trailhead was dry and the slope gentle and ticketed with yellow aspen leaves, and the vast fresh silence sounded in the sky. They walked as they had always walked on their backpacking trips, she then he, slow and steady up the path. They'd spoken only a little the night before, primarily because he had made himself one of his stone-cold promises that he would keep it light and tight and not get riled or ripped up. Every day since he had walked away from the jail had been a lesson in assembling himself, and he did not want to lose that. She was here; it was enough. They were no longer married. She was doing him a favor. He wouldn't get his hopes up; he had no hopes in this regard to get up. *You are hopeless, boy.* He whispered it. *Just go.* It was a fishing trip in September with a friend—a promise they'd made. All of this, sort of. He walked. He did not feel hopeless.

The first year, when she met him and was thrilled at the huge wild world they had captured at even the trailhead, she had hugged her arms in the evening chill and asked him why they went in September and not a warmer month.

"The summer must be splendid."

"It is, but there's nothing ruins a trip like a Boy Scout troop, all those little men with their merit badges. September is perfect. Frost in the morning, but perfect."

That first year she had kissed him as he cooked the pasta, and they slept in the tent together in separate sleeping bags, awake and aware in the small shelter. She'd brought a book, the poet Keats, and read him "Ode to Autumn" by her little flashlight.

"That's about got it," he said. "Did you put that to music?"

"I did."

"Was it for your boyfriend?"

"No. There was a boy who worked with a lot of Keats."

"Was he your boyfriend?"

"He was," Vonnie said, "but he had issues."

"Does that mean other girls?"

"He had us all," she said, and then she added what he wanted to hear. "But you've got me now."

"I won't be reading the Keats," Mack said. "But I know some stories."

"About the cannibal?"

"He wasn't a cannibal," Mack said. "But yeah."

The next day was a delirious hike up through the ancient trees, an entire mountain range made for two people. They were certainly the first people to hike these trails or so it seemed, even to Mack, who had never seen it this way before, and they invented each bend and turning and fallen log and rivulet, and they invented the air and the hours along with the day, ripe and yellow, something to walk through so they could camp early and make a small campfire for soup and a crust of bread. They took their time. He put up his cotton rope clothesline and hung his blue-and-green-striped dishtowel from it, a touch, and as she dunked her bread into the buttery tomato soup, she pointed and said, "Those sleeping bags zip together." Later, in the tent, every touch was a shock as they invented the embrace, and he put his hand on the inside of her thigh, polished and warm, and asked, "Are your legs okay?"

She held him and a minute later said, "This is the purpose of my legs, mister."

Now in the September sunlight they quietly walked the rocky trail that had been made wide by the horses of the summer outfitters and washed by rain and dried into an easy walk. Still they knew enough to watch their footing as the aspens gave way to the piñon pine and the spotty shade as they traversed the steep hillside and emerged into the first real mountain meadow, a hundred-acre field of sage and lupine and alpine daisies. The great splash of daylight after moving in the undulating tree shadows made them shield their eyes. Vonnie stopped at the edge of the park and he stepped up to her. They could see three dozen elk at the far edge, grand animals deep brown and small as dogs in the distance. Vonnie was breathing and he was breathing, two campers.

"Are you okay?"

"I haven't been out in a while; it's good." She put her hand on her sternum. "But I can feel it."

Now the elk were gone. "Let's go up and see if Clay has set up."

After dinner the night before, she had laid her pad and sleeping bag under the pines at the Cold Creek trailhead, and he asked her if she wanted in the tent.

"I'm good," she said. "I'm traveling light, but I've got a bivy sack if it gets cold."

"You want a hot rock?"

"I'm good."

"That's a great sleeping bag you've got there, lady," he said to her. "Kent get it for you?"

"He did."

"And the jacket?"

"Yes."

"He knows what he's doing with that gear. How is he?"

"You mean since your scrape?"

"Yes, I do. I apologized and paid for that."

"Kent is fine. Jackson's a good town for a lawyer."

"That's a terrible thing to say about a town, but it's deserved in the case of Jackson Hole."

"Mack, don't start. At all."

"Just tell me. Did he change your name?"

"He calls me Yvonne." He had planned on saying something to that, but when he heard it, he could not. He sat and pulled his boots off. Before he had crawled into his tent, he saw Vonnie go over and look under his truck, checking to see that he'd slid his familiar cooler there and then she stood in the luminescent dark and walked quietly over to the trailhead sign and retrieved her mail.

By the time they reached the top of the meadow, the last bees were out working the field, and Vonnie had rolled her sleeves in the sunshine. She walked to the primitive plank step-stile in the Forest Service fence and leaned there on the old weathered logs. It was a cross-timber fence built in the 1930s by the Civilian Conservation Corps, so huge and simple it would be there forever. Across the green lea they could see the large white lodge tent where the trail reentered the pines. Mack pointed. "He's in the same place." He could see that the familiar sight made Vonnie happy. "You want to do it?" Mack asked her.

"No, you like to."

"No, you—you don't get out much."

"Okay," she said, stepping up past him. "Hello the camp!" she called. "Hello the camp!" She smiled and made a megaphone of her two hands and called again, "May we! Approach! The camp!"

They saw Clay come out the canvas flap in his blue Utah State sweatshirt and wave. He hollered, "You better, Vonnie. Bring that rancher with you!"

"You better tell him it's Yvonne," Mack said.

"Leave it," she said, not looking back, her punctuation. "Let's go have some coffee and get the weather report." They helped each other step up and over the stile, and Mack followed Vonnie across to Clay's encampment. They leaned their packs against a big pine and went in the warm tent. Half the floor was pallet planking and half was green grass. Clay had two cots and a small woodstove. They all shook hands.

"Home sweet home," Vonnie said. She pointed at Clay's coffee cup, pen, open journal.

"And welcome to it," Clay said. "Sit down. Tell me what to write in the book; my journal suffers from a bit of the same old." He gathered his papers and set them on the one shelf.

"We didn't know if they'd hired a new kid."

"No, it's this old kid. Six years now. The money's good and I do love these hills."

"I forgot," Vonnie said and she went out and came back with a loaf of bread in a paper sleeve. "I brought you some sourdough from Lucy's in town."

"I'll take it," Clay said, "if you'll trade for coffee."

"With cream," she said. He lifted the blue enamel coffeepot from the steel stove surface and poured three tin cups, and he lifted a glass jar of half-and-half from his big igloo. "Who's coming this year?"

"It's all doctors from Chicago. Some of them from last year. Bluebride's bringing them four at a time."

"Where will they hunt?"

"We'll go south of here in the deep draws below Bellows and the three bald peaks. It's thick timber and makes a great outing. I've been this week clearing trails."

They sat at the wooden picnic table inside the tent.

"Anybody else above?" Mack asked.

"Nobody has come by here from Cold Springs. It's already snowed once. You guys going to Clark again? What is it? Ten years?"

"It's ten years," Mack said. "There's still fish in that lake. How's Deb?"

"She's good. That real estate license has made a difference for us, but who wants their wife dressing up every day showing strange men empty mansions? Who wants mansions anyway? But she's good."

"And Dougie?"

"Dougie thinks school is heaven on earth. We've got some bona-fide artwork on the fridge."

"And those," Mack pointed. There were sheets of crayoned squares and faces pinned to the tent wall.

"Those," Clay said.

"He's got the philosophy," Mack said. "People and houses. Have you heard any helicopters?" Mack asked him.

"No, sir. Are you thinking the vice president has gone fishing?"

"I'm just asking," Mack said. "I hope he isn't."

"That's the best coffee in Wyoming," Vonnie said. "I'm glad you're here."

"Stop by on the way down," Clay told them. "There'll be more. If I'm out with these guys, just come in and fire up some coffee. Stay the night if you need to."

Mack nodded at Clay's book. "Put us in the journal as two optimists," he said.

"I did already," Clay said. "Have fun."

The two hikers stepped out into the high-atmosphere sunshine and reclaimed the trail. Now it grew steep up the first hill, a series of long switchbacks. There were yellow blazes cut into the trees every thirty yards. One year on their fishing trip, it had snowed and they used the markings to pick their way down, tree by tree, arriving at the truck with the "coldest, wettest feet of all time," according to Vonnie, and when Mack handed her the warm ball of thick wool socks from the glove compartment, she came into his arms so fully that socks became their joke for foreplay. The blazes now were shiny yellow, coated with sap at summer's end.

An hour later, at the top, they discharged their packs and sat against them, legs out, breathing. From the promontory they could see south now, over the hills they'd climbed, seven ridgelines into the haze.

"One second," Vonnie said. "I'm going to pee." She went off into the trees.

Mack fished his BlackBerry from his pack pocket and dialed Yarnell's code. He entered: 9200 feet, W. of Crowheart 14 mi. Send reading. He had told the older man that it was a needle in a field of haystacks, and Yarnell had given him the device and said: "Yes, and this is how *it will find you*. If you get within a mile, the blue dot will light." Now Mack put it in his front pocket and stretched.

A minute later Vonnie came back, and they stood stiffly and packed up. They walked the ridgeline for half an hour, pacing carefully, and then descended in four long narrow switchbacks to Cross Creek, a rivulet that they could step over and where the trail ascended sharply, the first place a person would be happy to have a horse. Slow and even was their way. They'd known sprinters, friends who rocketed ahead, marching in a race, then stopping for five minutes at each turn, blowing, and it had been proven to all parties that slow and steady, slower and steady, was best and most workable through a long day. At the top of this ridge they sat again and ate apples, not talking, eating them all down to the seeds. Behind them two pikas began to call from the rock spill, piping their hopes for any dropped candy, apple cores.

"They remember us," Mack said.

"We're invaders," Vonnie said. "They're scared. Are they pikas?"

Mack piped back at the rocks, squeaking an imitation of their call.

"I thought they only lived in Utah," Vonnie said, picking up the old argument about the creatures.

"These two are following us, hope in their hearts," Mack said. "I'll leave them some trail mix."

"Leave them your knife and your flashlight, you woodsman."

They drank from their canteens and started walking again. This hill gave onto a gradual rise, and the forest grew thicker and darker.

Half an hour later in the deep shade, breathing, Vonnie stopped on the clay stairway of the trail and said, "This is your ptarmigan farm."

He looked up and knew the place. "It is. I'll get them someday. They'll be delicious."

"Don't go through it again."

One year they had come upon a dozen of the big white mountain birds walking up the trail ahead of them, almost tame it seemed, and Mack had tried to kill one by throwing shale. He could get ten feet and throw, missing by inches. The birds didn't panic but walked ahead. Dodos he called them, throwing and missing.

"There is a dodo here," she had said. As he hurled the stones at the unhurried assemblage, he described how he would cook the bird, how good it would be to have this savory fowl turning on a spit over a campfire. Then he described how he would fashion the elaborate spit out of green willows. Then after half an hour he gave up and the birds dispersed into the woods and let them pass.

"I'm grateful their extinction won't be pinned to me," he had said. "But I would have so happily made that spit."

Now they came to Broad Meadow, a huge open circle through which ran Cold Creek, a jewel. They could see snow in patches in the far shade. The trail went right to the creek, which was a pretty amber flow as wide as a road, a foot or two deep and glistening in the rocky sunlight.

"Don't even think about it, Mack."

"It's our trip," he said.

"It's a trip, but we're not doing any of that stuff. We're going to fish Clark and hike out, like we said. I'm glad you're feeling better," she said. "But no way."

He had always carried her across, from the first year when it had been a surprise to both of them. He had suddenly picked her over his shoulder in a fireman's carry, his hands clasped under her butt, and as he splashed through, she had laughed.

"Then you carry me," he said now. She walked upstream to the place where the stepping-stones were set and she walked carefully across and continued up the trail. He watched her for a moment. Then he knelt and washed his face in the cold water. He stood and took a deep breath and blew it out, and he followed her, keeping his old boots dry for the first time as he crossed Cold Creek.

They had married in the dooryard of the home place, before fifty friends and Vonnie's family and the three horses standing witness at the corral fence. A half hour before the ceremony his buddy Chester Hance had carried Vonnie off as the bridesmaids were having their pictures taken on hay bales in the barn. He'd lifted her sidesaddle onto Rusty as if for a photo, and then he'd mounted behind her and trotted up the famous horse trail into the aspens, waving his hat and hollering, "This lady has been abducted! She is too good for this horrid fate."

The young women hurried out of the barn, and they could

hear Vonnie's laughter as she struggled to say *help* and just laughed. Chester was a good rider. His colorful ransom note was discovered nailed to the barn door on a shirt cardboard. Half the letters were backward, and it occasioned another round of drinks. The entire scenario required Mack to ride up the trail backward on Copper Bob singing "Home on the Range." The horse knew what to do even with the man on wrong. The wedding party stood below as he disappeared still facing them, singing and happy into the trees. A moment later Chester hollered again and galloped into view. "I don't care if that gal is from the East Coast, she's more bobcat than any of the locals I know."

Someone called out, "As if you know any!" and the wedding party turned to see Mack and Vonnie ride down the trail together.

Sawyer Day, who was a justice, presided in his string bow tie, and they had a barbecue in the fragrant May day. Amarantha's husband Brett ran the pit, and she had set a fabulous buffet on sawhorse tables just off the porch. The fifty guests danced on the plank floor of the barn until midnight and then one o'clock; the band was jazz-bluegrass from Cheyenne, led by a guy who had been at school with Vonnie. They played the extra hour gratis as a wedding gift. As the trucks filed out the ranch road in the dark, full of friends calling back their jokes and good wishes, Vonnie and Mack sat on the old porch swing and it grew silent, except for the sounds of the house settling which hadn't felt such traffic for two or three years.

It was the moment between the old and the new worlds. His father would have sat up with them a minute like this on the porch; he liked the still night, the sleeping ranch. And then he would have stood, pivoting with his hand on Mack's shoulder, and

Mack that night felt the hand there, a blessing. His father would have stepped down into the dooryard on his way to the bunkhouse for this night, and still walking away, he would have touched his hat and raised his glass.

The horses looked at the couple from across the way. After half an hour in the night, Vonnie said, "I'm home."

"We'll keep this place," he said.

"Somehow," she said.

"There isn't much in making funky websites for the citizens of Jackson," he said. "We'll be land poor." For Mack the night yard was full of ghosts, and he knew he wasn't up to running a guest ranch. He could never greet the guests with the equanimity and grace—and real friendliness—his father mustered. He would feel a fraud.

"There's stuff," she said. "I'll teach."

"You married a ranch hand," he said.

"I did. I love that you're a hand," she said.

"And you're a heart," he said.

"Now we're really talking," she said. "Let's kiss." The three horses stood in the dark, their eyes unmoving. She whispered, "I didn't marry you for that horse. Let's go inside."

Now it was the warm high center of the day, and Mack and Vonnie ten feet apart moved up the trail, the sun on their necks. She stopped when they stepped into the beginnings of the rock field between the two verdant mountains. It was a mile of slumped talus through which the pack trail wound, a white line in the gray rock, struck there by horseshoes for uncountable years. The wind now blew north unimpeded, cuffing every loose sleeve. "Let's go up to the cairns and eat some lunch," he said.

"This has always been a weird place," she said, falling in behind him. For a while the world was rock and sky pressed by the wind. This was where the earth ended and the sky began, and the sky worked steadily for more. The trail was rippled and craggy and every step asked a balance, and Mack and Vonnie kept their arms out as if skiing. Mack's knees burned as they stepped over the top and found shelter from the sharp air. They sat at the crest against a sunny wall of the granite and looked ahead at the pitched green pine slopes of the massive upper valleys of the Wind River Range. South were the rocky towers of a grand cirque, Armitage, Bellow, and Craig, mountains that were in a score of picture calendars in Europe every year, mountains that had claimed a hundred lives, mountains with a dozen saucy nicknames each, the nicknames climbers give to dangerous places, wicked names and apt. North were the blankets of evergreens that ran aground at 11,500 feet and showed the round rocky promontories of the oldest mountains in Wyoming, striations of silver rock run and capped most of the year with snow at the summits.

"You get up here and you can see the planet again," she said.

"Our planet," he said.

"It's not ours."

"You don't know that. It looks like ours."

"You got any Vienna sausages?" she asked.

"I might," he said. "I've got this for you now." He handed her a round of fresh pita bread and then a thick slice of yellow cheddar. He peeled the lid from a tin of sardines in olive oil and lifted half of them onto her open bread with his pocketknife.

"All the food groups, thank you very much." They ate in silence. It was strange and pleasant out of the wind, and they could
now both feel the high chill of being sunburned.

Then the trail was packed dirt winding down the first western
slope, sage and berried-scrub and willows until they entered the
trees again at a place they called the Gateway because of the great
dead skeleton of a ponderosa standing over the trail, and high in
it on a huge branch strung an old withered pair of hiking boots
that had hung there through the years. Every time they saw
someone barefoot in Jackson, one of them would say, *I know
where her shoes are*, or *I know where that guy could get a pair of
boots*. The descent leveled off and they crossed a tributary of the
river, a stream that needed just a long step, and then the trail followed it gradually downhill. This became a valley that twisted
north and south, the creek bubbling as they went and they moved
apace. It was in this place that Mack always began to feel finally a
long way from his truck, from town, from all of it. He could
breathe; they were almost in.

From here Mack could see the switchbacks of the western trail
that led over the rim to Jackpine Lake, which was really three
lakes, where his father had taken him when he was ten. It had
been a great trip and a lesson, his father talking on the drive out
from town, saying, "What have we got now?"

"Sir?"

"How many horses?"

"Eleven." Mack knew them all by heart.

"Here," his father said, "right now?"

"None. No horses."

"And how many acres and ranches and buildings big and small, including tractors and saddles and tables and chairs and ladders and fences all totaled?"

Mack looked at his father's face as he drove. The faint smile. "None?"

"That's right, Mack. Just us and the truck and our gear, as I see it. You with me?"

"Yes, sir, I am."

At the trailhead they'd packed up and when they had climbed over the first hill, he'd said, "And how many trucks?"

"No trucks," Mack had said.

They'd camped at Jackpine, between the lakes, and the next day they'd walked around Larger Jackpine, and his father had said, "And now no tents, no pans, no stove."

"Daypacks and gear," Mack had said.

At the far end there was a rock spill onto which they walked. First they'd stashed their packs and stepped out carefully to fish.

Mack already knew the answers. "Our poles and some gear."

"That's about right," his father had said. "You got your knife, Mack?"

"My knife and some matches. Four flies."

"Well, this is very fine indeed," his father had said. "We're just about ourselves now. This is working perfectly. Three lakes and three days. We're getting down to some very fine mathematics." He swung his line free and gathered it back to cast. "Let's fish."

Mack had looked at the man, sleeves rolled, lifting a cast out onto the blue-brown mystery of the lake surface, and that line marked the known world from the unknown, and Mack wondered how he understood the depth of this little bay, how he knew where the fish were, how he knew everything he knew. The wondering seemed to hurt Mack's heart which he understood simply to be love, the aching desire to measure up, to master the mathematics.

The stream joined the Wind River in a muddy open glade criss-crossed with game trails, deer, elk, and moose tracks, a party. Mack walked the perimeter of the area and toed a small fist of bear scat. "This guy got into the gum," he said. "There's a bear full of tinfoil in these woods."

The sun was way west now and the shadows had changed, the day turned. They walked up along the Wind River to the two fallen logs, a bridge they'd used all the times, and they walked across the mountain river and sat down.

"Can you feel the altitude?"

"I think so. Let's have some water." Three deer came upstream and saw them and turned around and walked down.

"That's a nice pack Kent got you."

"I got it."

"For this trip?"

"For my trips."

"Kent backpacks?"

"He might."

"At two hundred seventy-five dollars an hour, it would be expensive hiking for that guy."

Vonnie rose and hefted her pack back into place high on her shoulders, cinching the waist strap. She led them away from the river on the old trail through the pines. A mile later she stopped at the rim of the upper bowl. Mack joined her and they looked down into the wilderness. "Where are we going to camp?"

"We always camped at Valentine." This was their neighborhood.

"Where are we camping today?"

Mack lifted his chin. "Let's go over there," he said. "I know where there's a ring of stones and some firewood."

Valentine Lake was a twenty-acre heart of silver blue rimmed to the edge by pines and red sandstone. They came over the low ridge and saw it set out as if invented this morning. Circling west they stepped up the stony terrace to the rock porch where they'd been before. It had the advantage of a level place for the tent and the boulders made a kind of room, good for sitting and leaning the packs. The fire ring was still in place, remarkable in that it was unused; this wasn't on any trail. They had gathered the six rocks, each the size of an unabridged dictionary, ten years before and set them here on earth above the lake. Mack shrugged off his pack and leaned it against one of the boulders. He marched off into the trees, counting them to ten and finding the steel wire oven rack where he'd hung it. Over three stones it made a perfect cook stove.

"We are golden," he said, returning.

Vonnie hadn't moved, her pack still on. Now she walked to the perimeter of the campsite, her hands clasped behind her, a strange look on her face. "This is such a bad idea."

He had seen this face before, almost a year ago. He said, "Let's get some firewood." The day had broken on the evening's clouds, and the surface of the lake was a million coins in the breeze. She looked at Mack and he stopped.

"How's Trixie?"

He folded his arms.

"No, how is she."

He knew to stand and face it, but it was against the grain. "Her name was Trisha."

"Trixie."

Mack waited, but he knew to be silent was to lie and he was done with that. "And she's gone. You know that."

"Oh, what happened, big boy? Did you lie to her?"

"Don't, Vonnie. I mean, you don't need to."

"Don't."

He had resolved in his bitter extremity to say things as they were, not to duck or feint. It was one of the hardest things he had ever done, and it hurt every time before the relief descended. He hated to have this conversation here, above the lake in their camp, but he would do it. "Trisha is gone. I made a mistake. A series of them."

"Just one series of mistakes?"

"Vonnie."

"Did you just lie to her?"

"Don't."

"No, I won't. It's a stupid question, no? To ask a liar if he lied."

"Vonnie. Let's get some wood."

"Liar. A lying liaristic lie-maker."

"I stopped lying."

"Oh, when, ten minutes ago? How does a liar stop lying?"

"Vonnie."

"Do they remove something?"

"Vonnie."

"Yvonne. And let's not get wood. No fire. Let's just go up to Clark Lake." She was crying now and her pack was shaking a little as she stood. "And catch a fish and get out of these fucking mountains."

"You love these mountains."

"I used to." Her pack trembled. "But they're full of liars now. You even ruined the mountains."

"Do you want to camp someplace else?" She didn't answer but turned and stood looking at the corrugated lake in the mountain twilight. "I'm sorry, Vonnie." He now too felt it a mistake, all the mistakes. "This was the wrong spot, all wrong. I'm sorry."

"Valentine Lake," she said. "Go get some wood."

The wind was steady, but the small fire bent and flourished, and he cooked the tomato soup as always and burned the bread on his long fork so they could dip strips into their bowls. The fire helped. Vonnie took off her boots and wore her camp moccasins, sitting by the fire. They'd unpacked and Mack had set his tent. Vonnie was reading, holding the book flat to catch the light.

"How's the school?" he asked.

"It's going well; every time they cut the music program some rich parent steps up. Somebody gave us a grand piano, but we don't have a room for it, so now they're building a room. There's a lot of money in that town, but it only comes out in certain ways."

"A grand piano."

"Yeah, and Kent started a board that does fund-raising."

"He's got to be good at that. And he gave the school a car."

"He did."

Mack had wiped out the bowls and wrapped them in the dish-towel. "Did he not want you to do this?"

"Of course he didn't. He hates you. You should have never fucked with his car."

"I shouldn't have done anything I did this past year, Vonnie, but breaking the most expensive windshield in Jackson was as pure an act as ever I did."

"You were drunk?"

"I was drunk for, let's see, just about five months." Mack turned to her and held open his hands. "I'm sorry, Vonnie. Sorry. But more, I'm done with it. I'm done with desperation. I was as lost as you get."

"How was jail?"

"That is a great question. You always said I was in my own way with my pride, remember that?"

"You were."

"I was. Jail fixed that. I'm not proud anymore. Jail is jail and I had weeks of it and those weeks were the same as a lot of weeks last year. I'm all even all over town, except for two more apologies and the bills. Bills and three more apologies, but I'll get them."

"Who's on the ranch?"

"Jessups. He was going to get sheep, but as far as I can see they're just living there."

"Do you get a decent rent?"

"Decent minus the horses, the upkeep. I'm a little negative, but I'm working on some projects."

"Did Yarnell come through?"

"Sort of." Mack set sticks into the small fire. The last daylight was trading around from the rocky towers, and the gloaming would last half an hour. It took the darkness a long time to fill.

"Kent says you're tight with Yarnell and that Yarnell is the enemy, a crook."

"He'd know."

"He'd know before you'd know."

"Well, I've got some projects is all."

"You could sell it all and just go."

"I could and where would I go? Where do people go, Vonnie? San Diego? My knees are too bony. This is where I go."

"You're fighting the whole county."

"I just want to keep the place. Stay straight and do what I can to keep the place."

"The bank?"

"The bank is the bank. They were with me and now they're deciding. You want me to sell so you can get that money?"

"Mack, did you look at the letters?" He had the five ivory envelopes unopened in his father's rolltop.

"Not yet. I'm sure they explain your position. They are beautiful envelopes, Vonnie. That guy has some bona-fide stationery. My theory is that beautiful envelopes are full of terrible news. I can wait if you can."

"You are still proud. And you are dumb as a stone."

"Don't let the stones hear you talking that way."

There had been a dozen ups and downs before Mack really went down. He had lived forever at the edge of his money and he was tired of it. After they were first married, he had to rent the place out and he and Vonnie took a place in Driggs, across the border, an old refurbished trailer at the end of a road for the grayest year of his life. At first it was right. He could feel the money they were saving, positive four hundred dollars a month, almost, working the mortgage along, but the stupid place was built into the hillside and cold at all times and actually not even level, but they were in love and poor and so fine, but then they wore out poor and they did some damage to love. Her parents offered help and they took some, and it stung Mack and he took the stinging as a weakness, but he could not turn it into anything good.

He remembered one day when she came out of the little tin bath in just her shirttails holding up a pair of her underwear to the light and he could see them worn thin and she was laughing, saying, "This is us in the glory days, my ass a millimeter from the world. If I have to go to the hospital, change my drawers first, please. Promise me. Go to Woolworth's and get me a highwaist pair of whities before they operate."

She was laughing and laughing, and so he swallowed it all and laughed too, the poor ranch owner a millimeter away from losing the deed. But it hit him and was a seed of his desperation. He was working odd jobs, one in a bookstore drugstore/drive-thru liquor in Driggs, and she was teaching piano out at the ranchsteads. In the spring, when they moved to Jackson and took a two-bedroom townhouse a hundred dollars over their budget, the farmer they had rented from hauled their terrible trailer out to his summer house and buried it for a septic tank. They had laughed about that too. Seven years ago or six, he forgot.

Now he stood up. "You want to fish? There's still some light."

"It's cold and I'm tired," she said, "but yeah."

"Okay, let's go down." They geared up in camp and walked down fifty feet to the lake. Three boulders protruded into the water, each as big as a bus, and they stood downwind and cast into the mirrored sections along the shore.

"How's your fly selection," she asked, an old joke. There was no selection. He only had one size of big woolly caddis, but he had twenty of the things.

"Perfect," he said. "They like these bugs." He had clipped on a red bobber and threw it thirty yards straight out, the wind ballooning his line as it fell.

"A bobber?" she said.

"I like to use it once and put it away." The light failed imperceptibly. A mote across the lake became an eagle, a crescent that looped and landed alongside another in the top branches of the skeleton of a massive dead piñon. Vonnie glassed them with her binoculars.

"Somebody's been to REI."

"These are good," she said, handing them to him.

He was surprised at the lensing. He could see the throat feathers ripple. "It's mother and daughter."

"You don't know that."

"They're women," he said. "See how calm they are." He gave

her back the new glasses. "I'll be back," he said, clipping his rod with a stone. Mack walked back up to camp and looked down on Vonnie lifting her line for another set. He powered the Black-Berry and dialed the window. He'd have to get within a mile to catch any signal from the missing part, and he didn't know if that was sightline. The odds were crazy. He typed in: 10.5K Valentine. Send. He turned it off and looked at the device and put it back in his pocket. It was an uncomfortable lump, just like the whole deal.

He'd been out of jail two weeks when Yarnell called. They had stayed in touch through the years with Mack doing short spot contract jobs, softcore hacking, for Yarnell for cash from time to time. It was a weird call, but they were all weird; whenever Mack was with Yarnell, he felt it in his gut. It was going to be trouble, but Mack felt he deserved it. And there was always money. Yarnell said to meet at the Tropical, the funky bowling alley in Jackson. Walking over there in the dark, Mack thought, this has got to be the low, meeting a crook in the bowling alley. He knew it was his father talking, and Mack straightened up. He'd lost weight in jail and he cinched his tooled belt to the old notch. You're not fit to choose your company, he reminded himself. You've got to make something work. He's going to say something and you're going to do it, good or bad. Then in the summer night he spoke aloud, "Just who are you, cowboy?"

The bowling alley had been at the thin tail end of its heyday when Mack was in high school, and then it slid into sleazy ruin and now it had been washed twice and was half smart and half tony, a place for the slumming realtors and tourists from Germany and Japan. The sign was a beauty: the big white neon bowling pin lit three times in a spin, rotating in jerks: up, over, upside down; up, over, upside down. It hummed as Mack walked under.

Yarnell signaled him from the gravel parking lot, and Mack walked over and climbed into the black Land Rover. Mack had resolved to let the older man speak first.

"You had some trouble," Yarnell said. "Sorry."

"Yeah," Mack said. It was an effort now. "Did you hear it from Chester?"

"He didn't say much, but yeah."

"I'm out."

As always, Charley Yarnell looked polished, his gold wire glasses and his broad forehead. He was wearing a two-hundred-dollar pink-checked shirt with a silver pen in the embroidered pocket. Mack had seen such shirts at the ranch. You saw a dozen any Saturday night in Jackson. Brokers wore them on western holidays.

"Anything I can help with?"

"The place is still not for sale."

"I know, son, but it won't need to be if the mortgage folds. I'll just step up and claim the pretty place."

Mack had his hand out almost to Yarnell's chest. "No *son*, Charley. Let's just talk."

"What happened to you?"

"Too much to say. But recently I got myself arrested breaking a windshield right over there about six streets. I was drunk and thought I had a reason. There was worse stuff that they didn't catch me for." It always cleared his head to admit this. "Look, I can get out of your car right now." He turned to Yarnell and saw he was being studied. There was something about him that Yarnell liked, and Mack understood it to be the weak places.

"I got a job for you, if you want. Some money, which you need."

"I'm open. I expect it's not computers."

"It's an airplane. Remember the drones from my place?"

"I do." A few summers before Mack had driven out to Yarnell's place sixty miles west. It looked like a ranch from the road, but behind the house and the barn and the toolshed were twenty acres of winter wheat and then a narrow asphalt landing strip and four small hangars. You had to duck your head in two of them. Charley Yarnell had two Cessnas, one a blue twin engine, and a two-man grasshopper helicopter under a canvas awning. But he took some time showing Mack his set of a dozen drones, little gray things with single jet engines with air intakes the size of liter bottles. "This is the future," he said. "This is the money." He could get them to take off in sixty feet, a ninety-pound aircraft, and he ran them from handhelds and from the computers in one of the buildings. "They're hardwired for this strip," he said. "Latitude, longitude, and elevation." He pointed to the control panel along the fuselage. "All I put in is the time to touchdown and the wind speed."

Yarnell had Mack's old friend Chester working for him and the whole little spread was squared away nicely. Chester had been in high school with Mack and he waved from the small hangar and pushed one of the little planes out onto the paved lane with a long T-bar. When he came over, he took Mack's hand and asked, "How's that place, cowboy?"

"Rented out for now," Mack said.

"It's a tough country on ranches," Chester said. "You ought to get back out there and run it." Yarnell stepped over and Chester handed him the control unit.

"I might. And now you're a pilot?"

"Yes sir. I went to airplane school," Chester said. "You'd like flying."

"There's too many mountains in my life to put an airplane in it."

Yarnell handed Mack the control to examine and took the T-bar from Chester and straightened out the little plane, handing the bar back to Chester without looking.

"This gentleman has some airplanes. Some don't need a pilot; that right there tells you how hard flying is."

A bright blue six-wheel tank truck entered the far yard. Chester stepped up and took Mack's hand again. "I'm glad to see you. I'm going to get over and take delivery on some fuel. Say hey to Vonnie and get back with your horses, you cowboy."

"Will do, Chester."

Yarnell showed Mack the hand controller for the aircraft and then led him over to four white Adirondack chairs in the shade of the hangar. He had Mack press the switch and then hold the red button which ignited the jet, more of a hiss than a roar. Yarnell took the controller back and used the simple joystick to send the plane forward in a sudden rush, like a thrown thing, instantly in the sky and a moment later out of sight. They had coffee for twenty minutes there and Mack scanned the bulbous cumulus cloudbank running along the blue-sky horizon like a hedgerow for the craft the whole time. Yarnell had made a show of putting the controller on the ground.

"There," the man said, pointing.

Mack saw the gray dot again, remarkably small, now descending slowly like a toy and banking at the end of the strip for a turn, coming in for a landing in soft bumps with the engine off. "Hands off," Charley said.

"Where'd it go?"

Yarnell looked at him. "You tell me. I loan these to the government."

"Don't they have their own?" Mack had asked.

"That there is a mystery," Charley had said. "I wanted you to see what we're doing is all." Mack looked across at Chester atop the fuel truck with his wrench and he did feel a little better about the whole deal.

In Yarnell's Rover in the parking lot of the Tropical, Mack asked, "What's the job?"

"We lost part of something. It fell from a plane. It's about the size of a book."

"In the mountains?"

"In the Winds."

"Some kind of secret?" Mack said.

"Some kind."

"Is it radioactive?"

"No. It's too hard to explain," Yarnell said. "But it's like a trigger, a fingerprint. And they need it. It's the linchpin, the prototype."

"There's a new drone."

"There is."

Mack asked, "This trigger. Whose is it?"

"Ours," Yarnell said.

"*Ours* as in *us*," Mack said. "Who?"

"It's worth ten thousand dollars to you, if you can hand it to me." Mack watched the big bowling pin tumble through its stations. Behind it the night was lit by the bar lights of Jackson, and the outline of the two-story town was cut against the mountain. Looking over the buildings had always confounded Mack. It wasn't just Jackson; it was any town. There was something wrongheaded and sad about the venture to him, something that didn't fit. He could abide it, but the clock was ticking.

"What if it's all broke apart? It's going to be broken up."

"If I knew that for certain, that too would be worth some money."

"Who else wants it?"

"I don't know. I don't know who knows about this."

"I mean like the Chinese? Are they going to be crawling around the hills?"

"I can't imagine," Yarnell said.

"Who else have you hired?"

"No one."

"And you can't say one thing."

"That would not be safe," he said.

"Who else in this part of the country knows about it?"

"I don't know."

Mack was thinking as fast as he could. "When did they drop it?"

"Two days ago."

"Is there a signal, a GPS?"

"No. Yes, but weak. A mile max. I know the flight line and the hour it went missing. This is a private experimental aircraft and they don't want to lose that piece or leave it out there. It's bigger, much bigger than the stuff I showed you." He unfolded the USGS map. There was a red oval that covered the entire diagonal. "We may not find it, any trace, and that's worth five grand, but you've got to look. We need this." Yarnell opened his face in the sincere way that great liars can and Mack knew that face.

"I don't know where it is," he said. "I need you. It's a long shot, but you know the country."

"Some," Mack said. After a minute he added, "I'm taking Vonnie."

"I thought . . ."

"You thought what about Vonnie, Mr. Yarnell? She's a friend of mine. Is it at all dangerous or just a walk in the big woods?"

"A walk," Yarnell said. He opened the glove box and pulled out a packet of hundreds. Mack saw his own hand go out and take the money. Twenty bills. "A start. Good luck. Go bowling and have a sandwich. You know how the BlackBerry works. It should be a walk in the woods."

With the money in his pocket, Mack had no position from which to speak. He pushed open the door with some effort and slid to the ground. In the last year every time somebody had handed Mack a sheaf of money, it had been freighted with shame and this was no different. He could taste it. Mack heard the vehicle back and drive out through the gravel. He walked up under the humming sign and entered the carpeted auditorium which smelled of beer and echoed with muffled crashing.

———

Now the wind came up as if charged by the great shadows, and with the sun gone, the cold gathered. Vonnie always fished until he called it; she wouldn't quit first. His bobber was bright in the lake, something as out of place as it could be. "They're in here," he said, "but let's leave them tonight. It's chilly." The far hill had collapsed into darkness and the birds were gone.

"One more," she said, drawing an elegant arc with her flyline and tipping the fly in the lee of the rocky bank forty feet farther. She reeled in and turned to him. There was a smile on her face, and he saw it. Fishing worked. It was something that still worked.

In their campsite Mack fed up the fire and banked it with a little log windward in case they got up in the middle of the night and needed to refire for tea or cocoa, and he sat in the tent and pulled on his sweatpants. He felt like a man washed up on the beach after trying to drown himself. His shoulders hurt. How could he have made such mistakes? Ten years and here he was in a tent alone. He groaned, a habit he disliked in himself, but it was better than the swearing that had taken him months to stop. Somewhere getting in his car and he'd say, Fuck me, and look around and have to silently take it back. He drew a deep breath. He could feel the altitude headache like a tight hat. He heard noises but they were nothing; the first night way up like this and it always seemed the woods were full of traffic. He climbed out of the tent again and erected his clothesline in the dark and clipped the blue and green towel to it with a wooden clothespin. He always had clothespins. Vonnie had bedded against the windward rock in the pine needles. "You want in the tent?"

"I'm good," she said, crawling in her bag. "This goes to twenty below."

"That's plenty," he said. "You won't need a hot stone." She gave him a look. He'd burned his sleeping bag with a rock plucked from the campfire on their third trip. "You want a story?"

"Oh Mack, not tonight."

"Those were fine eagles," he said. "I wonder if we'll see our owl."

"It's not ours," she said.

"It's ours," he said.

Day Three

At dawn the bowl of mountain sky grew from gray to gold in one minute like a sail filling with wind, and when Mack looked up from where his first flames bit the tinder pile he was working, vertigo crossed his vision like a cloud. It was strange to have moments like these erase his worries, but they were only moments. The little fire grew, pure and smokeless and he fed it twigs and now bigger branches that he had broken last night. His frying pan sat on the duff beside him already greased with a finger of butter, and he shook the quart jar of pancake mix with his left hand. The old tin coffeepot stood full of water on a rock. The air was sharp in the mountain shade and only the far western rock-tops were silver in the sun. The frost was furry on his tent and Vonnie's form was printed on the top of her sleeping bag in brilliant ice crystals. She was still sleeping. Mack laid two small logs on the blaze and crossed them with two, set down the jar in the dirt, and walked through the trees fifty yards and leaned against a dead tree there with his BlackBerry. No signal, it read. The cold collared him. Valentine Lake below was now one single sheet of gray glass. In the far coves he could see the white line of the ice fringe growing a foot and sometimes two out from the bank.

He watched rings begin to appear around the perimeter, ten, then a hundred, as fish tested the world. He'd seen the surface flies yesterday, almost invisible tiny white gnats that trout preferred to his ungainly homemade fuzzballs. He'd never operated at the keen center of fly-fishing, the way the guides and dandies did in Jackson. He'd seen their product, so precise and elegant it seemed like watchmaking, and the flies themselves looked like a fabulous meeting of jewelry and semiconductors. He had always tied one fly, brown and coarse and big as a whisk broom, his father used to say. Grab a couple and sweep the barn. But, and this made his father smile too, they worked. He didn't get the little ones or the smart ones or any fish in a reserve river that had seen worldly equipment thrown his way night and day all season, but Mack caught keepers who laid out in the hungry places. That was the whole secret: fish where they haven't seen you before. He tried again: no signal. The sun now was crawling down the hills toward them, and the sky was what his father called toothache blue, unreal and shocking, which would last for twenty minutes and then blond out with the sun. Vonnie still hadn't moved, so Mack laid more wood on the fire and set the grill on the stones and the black iron pan on that until the butter started to skate. He lifted the warm pan and poured in four dollops of his pancake mix and they spread into pretty circles and fixed.

"I'm cooking," he said to the blue sleeping bag. He saw her squirm and roll around and her face appeared.

"Morning," she said.

"Hi, Vonnie."

"Here, wait," she said and she disappeared again into the sleeping bag. "I brought something." She threw him a foil pouch of ground Hagen's coffee. It was warm.

"How's Mrs. Hagen?" he asked.

"She's okay. Her son came back from Portland and he's doing the baking now; they're going to run Starbucks out of the county. I brought some of their bear claws too, for later."

"Oh, that's good."

"I saw you at the funeral."

"I saw you at the funeral with Kent. He didn't represent Mr. Hagen too, did he?"

"No, just friends. Now look the other way."

"What?" He looked at her, the recognizable sleep face, his favorite face.

"Look away."

"You sleeping naked?"

"How I sleep is not your beeswax."

Beeswax. He packed the coffee basket with coffee and assembled it again and set it on the grill.

"You found the coffeepot."

"Yeah, I finally looked for it. You want it?" he said. "It's half yours."

"No, I just want some coffee. Those your buttermilk pancakes?"

"They are."

"Things are looking up," she said. "Now look away."

"I am, goddamnit. I don't need provocation."

"What?"

"I can't use provocation."

"Is that what your doctor said?"

He turned back to where she lay in the sleeping bag, her face on him. He could see her pants rolled for a pillow. "My doctor's remarks are none of your beeswax, to use the technical term. At this fucked-up point in my life I don't need to see a naked woman in the woods."

"You've already seen it," she said. "Now turn away. It's not all that provocative."

"Vonnie, goddamn, run off and pee and get dressed and stop provoking me." He could hear her rustling and stepping away, and he looked fixedly at the steam as it emerged from the coffeepot and the bubbles rising at the edges of the pancakes, and he reached around in his galley sack for the powdered cream and the jar of honey so he could warm it a little on one of the square stones in the old fire ring. There was a small plastic bottle of maple syrup. Vonnie came back in a blue plaid Pendleton and Levi's, buckling her belt. She was barefoot and sat on one of the red sandstones at the perimeter and brushed off the bottom of her feet and pulled each sock on carefully and tied her boots double.

"It's warming up," she said. "Do you like your doctor?"

"Here's some coffee, dear," he said, handing her one of the old mugs. She bent and dropped a spoon of honey into the steaming coffee, stirring it. "I like everybody now," Mack said. "It's the new me." He turned the cakes one by one in the pan, showing them browned perfectly. "Let's eat all this and decide where we're fishing." The sun clipped their campsite and continued revealing the valley, rising over the now-blue lake. The lake would change all day. "Those Pendleton wools are ninety dollars," he said. She looked at him as a challenge. "Nothing," he said. "It looks good on you and they make a good shirt. I hear."

"How far is Clark?" she said. "Not five miles, right?"

"Come on, Vonnie. We'll get there. This is a trip; this is the last trip. Let's fish. Let's not rush this."

"Three miles?" she said.

He pointed northwest. "Three miles." He slid the flapjacks from the pan onto paper plates and handed her a fork.

"Smells good."

"Use that syrup."

"Got any cheese?" He reached and carved out a slice of the cheddar onto her breakfast, and he watched her sandwich it up and stripe an X of syrup over it all. Her mouth was full and she said to him: "It's good. Let's go up to the meadow and fish the Wind by the old bridge. It will be warm there and it will make a good day, right?"

He watched her eat and then he ate as well. They walked out from Valentine and joined the trail again, climbing up and down through the trees until they reached the main mountain valley. From there half a mile in an easy ascent, they stepped into a place simply called Deer Park on the maps, a long twenty-acre meadow through which ran the stream. Meadow willows lined the river and made it difficult to get down to fish, but there were spots. It was hard not to fish the first place; it was always hard not to fish the first place. The oldest story. The water was clear, the brown rocky bottom vivid and mesmerizing, amber and a magnified gold. Vonnie led them on the trail through the grass and wild-flowers to where their trail met the township trail which ascended from near Dubois. There was a log bridge here and on the far side three big logs had been drawn together as benches. They crossed and sat on the warm worn wood. They were going to prepare their tackle. Mack's heart was up, working the way it did when he felt he was fully in the woods. They had the whole world now, east west north south, and the river was singing. There was always stuff at this crossroads, an ammo box of broken fishing gear, swivels, rod tips, sometimes a pocketknife, but today there was a new spill of gum wrappers and six or seven beer cans that hadn't been there two days, cigarette butts, still white, tobacco crumbs, footprints of running shoes.

"Let's not stay here," Mack said. "That bear is going to want his litter."

"Okay. What?"

He toured the lakes in his head: Double, Native, White, Chester, others. "Let's go up to Spearpoint. You can fish from the glacier. Two miles."

"No trail," she said.

"Right, but we can find it; we did before."

"Wasn't that an accident, though?"

"I can find it."

It was sunny and early in the day, and Vonnie said, "Lead on."

They continued down the Wind trail, paralleling the stream where it rushed, crossing the tributaries that fed in from the west. At each one Mack stopped and surveyed the hill. There was no trail to Spearpoint, but a creek flowed out of it and came down this way. They hadn't been up there for five years, and all he remembered was that the outflow was subterranean, flowing under a broken rock sheet most of the way down. At the third feeder Mack turned and led them uphill through the small pines and the scree, back and forth, crossing and recrossing the rivulet until it vanished into the hillside, and he knew they were going the right way. They came out of the trees onto a hill of rock lined with lichen above the treeline, the rocks looking smashed and fitted, and they ascended this shoulder for half a mile until they came to a barren plain before a rocky cirque that like the entire series along the mountain crest could have been called the Throne. The hidden stream still clucked below them, sounding like a muted conversation. They could see the glacier at the far end of the field and then walking up ten more feet, the blue sheet of Spearpoint Lake appeared like a forbidden secret, like it had been trying to hide. The whole world now was only sky, rock, and water. Small lichens grew like coral here and there between the rocks, but there wasn't a tree or a bush bigger than a hand. Mack and Vonnie stood on the flat sandstone and listened to the creek gurgle through the rocks beneath their feet. They were both arrested by the place and they stood side by side, breathing. Vonnie stepped forward carefully onto the plates of rock, each one set like a puzzle piece in the mountain. There was no bank. Water lipped rocks in one seamless field.

"I remember this," she said. "We caught fish here and you said it felt funny taking them because you didn't know how they got here."

"Look around," he said, grinning at the remarkable place. "Do you?"

She pointed down into the gray brown depths which were run with corridors of sunlight, and two brown trout went by at a depth they couldn't measure.

"This is good," she said. "I do love these mountains." She skirted the lake on the south side stepping easily onto the flattened rocky hillside. Mack turned his back to her and lifted the BlackBerry. He dialed Yarnell's code and the screen opened: 2pm Wed Overflt. Will send.

"What are you doing?" Vonnie called back.

"Counting my cigarettes," he said.

"You don't smoke."

"I smoke," he said. "Dr. Diver said I could smoke. I just haven't started." He put the BlackBerry in his pocket and followed her toward the glacier. They had to walk up and around the huge ice block to get atop and from the rocky crest at the western edge Vonnie stopped again and looked into the newly revealed vista. It was impossible to say how far they could see, and so much of it was lost in layers of haze.

"Where's Jackson?" she said. "Can you feel the earth turning?"

The wind in the saddle was steady, the heated air from its ascent up the sunny slopes suddenly at the summit and spilling into the high mountain valley, and the sun was warm on their shoulders. They walked up the ridge and onto the dirty glacier which was banked in the eastern lap of the rocky peak and curved an easy crescent like a half-moon from the rock face out in a frozen cantilever over the lake. From here they could see why it was called Spearpoint, the tip at the other end where the outflow departed. The glacier was riddled with soot and the walking was sure-footed, the surface neither slush nor ice. "This is all airliners," she said, kicking at the dirt.

"Probably," he said. Smog, coal fire, airliners. They stepped down to the lake edge of the glacier, now twenty feet above the surface of the lake, and the curtains of sunlight ran into the water a hundred feet. They could see fish moving at every level.

"If you can see them, you can't catch them," she said. His old saw.

"You can catch them," he said. "Don't let them see you."

She took his arm above the elbow. "Mack, thanks. I'm glad I came."

He stood on the small glacier on Spearpoint Lake. "You know, I am too."

They sat on their jackets, cross-legged, and Vonnie unfolded her flies, which were wrapped in a pocketed fleece case. "My god," Mack said, looking at the array. "We're rich." There were forty flies, some the size of capital letters in the Bible and some as big as dimes, all of them four-color, three-material masterpieces.

"He puts the eyes in." Vonnie pointed to the red dots and the gold dots on the tiny flies.

"I am admiring his handiwork," Mack said. "Kent's got a touch." He pointed to a dun-feathered fellow with a red stripe. "Use this guy, I think." He looked out over Spearpoint, a dozen moving shadows therein. "Try him. He will speak to the lonely fish below us. And I am going to throw this until they respond." He pulled one of his linty caddis from his jacket pocket. They sat in the coarse snow and tied up, cinching and clipping for ten minutes. When they looked up again into the larger world, they marveled again at the stony bowl of mountains, five peaks purely above the treeline, and they took great breaths of the unlimited air. Vonnie stood and measured, arm back and then forward, arcing her line in a full billow out like a compass so that it snaked down and kissed the surface and ran out slowly, pulling the airborne fly on its invisible leader fifty feet from shore where it landed in a silver dot which became a ring and then two on the mystery of the water. Mack stepped down the glacier thirty feet and drew his cast shorter, the big fly almost splashing where it hit. Then they both saw something remarkable. Three fish darted from the dark, zigging left and right, urgently ascending through the lighted panes of water, unmistakable in their intent, two racing toward Vonnie's fly, a wonder, and both splashing there, the first sound in the cirque of the mountains that wasn't the wind or the faint harmonics of intercontinental planes. As they struck, the other trout took Mack's fly, smacking his tail like a shovel, racing away with his prize.

"Holy shit," Vonnie said. Their rods bent and bobbed, both reels giving line in these first moments. They had been taken by the place, the desperate beauty of fishing from the glacier so far above the water, and they hadn't considered this part. They'd made a mistake, and it was apparent in that first second. The glacial ledge was still fifteen feet above the lake, too far for landing anything.

Mack gave line and walked the edge quickly marching, his rod aloft around the edge of the snowfield to where, when it tapered to ten feet, he could slide off onto the rocky bank in a small cascade of the old snow. Now he adjusted his drag and reeled it tight again, the fish fighting and the rod flexing as if alive. He was good now, but the fish was out sixty yards. Vonnie had trouble though, her fish had plunged and she was stuck up in the snow. "I can't get around there," she said.

"Wear him out," Mack said. "I'll come back when I get this guy." For every three turns he could take, the fish took one back. "Wish I had some lemon drops," Mack said. His father always had a pocket of the hard candy and told Mack that a good fish would last as long as the candy did in the boy's mouth—and no chewing. Mack held the rod in one hand and rolled one shirtsleeve and then changed hands and rolled the other. His father would stand back when a fish was on, never beside him as if to take the rod; Mack was on his own. He'd give him a lemon drop and back away, saying a couple of times, "Nice work, son."

The sun was hot now. He could see Vonnie's line angled out into the lake where the big fish did what he wanted. Eventually he worked his fish in, horsing him more than he'd like, always it seemed at the edge of snapping the line. Back and forth in the red shallows the big brown trout swam, frantic when he saw the man. Mack let him go each way five times and then lowered his pole almost to the water and reeled in, lifting and taking the line in his hand and backing straight away, dragging the trout onto the wet rock shelf and then farther onto the dry sandstone, where it twisted and jumped in a tangle of line. Mack got his fingers in the gills, dropped the fish, grabbed him again and lifted him into the air. It was an eighteen-inch brown, heavy as a single muscle. Holding him between his knee and the rock, Mack tapped him sharply on the head twice with the handle of his knife and the fish shuddered and stopped. Mack carried his tackle and the fish, still hooked, back into the rocky lichen and laid it all there. He had to circle again away from the lake to the rocky summit to mount the glacier and he joined Vonnie where she stood as if her line were seized by the lake itself. "Let's try to get down," he said.

"He's too tight." Every step she took bent her pole further.

"Let's wait, just wait."

There would be some slack and she'd take it and then give it back. Slack, reel, yield.

"Maybe they both took it," he said. "It looks like two fish."

"Mack," Vonnie said. "Just one, but he's worthy."

"You want a granola bar?" he asked her.

"Not really."

"It's from Hagen's."

"You went there too?"

"I'm not as dumb as I look."

"Yes you are." He opened the homemade biscuit and held it before her mouth. She took a bite and said through the chewing, "Did you get bear claws too?"

"I did."

"We're at capacity with baked goods." He took a bite of the bar and then held the canteen so Vonnie could drink.

"You got a headache?"

"Very small, but we're up here." There was some slack and she took it and more and she reeled in.

"He's coming in. He's swimming under the shelf."

Vonnie reeled steadily. "Can you see him?"

"No." Then Mack saw something and it was the fish's shadow in the water and then the trout near the surface. "He's too close." Vonnie snugged the line and the fish responded, leaping and in that second seeing the world, the two people in the white snow, it twisted with every ounce of itself, and the fish swam away, the fine broken leader trailing from its mouth. They could see him race down, diving through the bladed sunlight of the lake water, and then stall and settle again as if nothing had happened.

Vonnie looked at Mack, her face blank and then he saw the old smile emerge.

"Fish," she said.

They were at the wild rough top of the world.

She reeled in and they gathered their jackets and walked back as they had come to step off the glacier and go around to the lake.

"How long will our footprints be in that thing?" she asked.

"Eons," he said. "It's going to confuse the anthropologists in the distant future. 'It looks like one of them had real expensive boots,' " Mack said, " 'but what were they doing up here?' " She reached into his shirt pocket and withdrew the rest of the Hagen granola bar.

When they got to the lakeside, she admired Mack's fish. "You want to get yours?" he said.

"I better," she said. They walked out the rock shelf and looked into the water. The fish held and their shadows held. She lifted her binoculars and sighted and said finally, "There he is with a foot of my leader."

"Let's hope he's still pissed off and hungry and can beat these other guys to the punch," Mack said, pointing, "Set your fly out here so it's between him and the sun. You want a cup of tea?"

"Yeah, make some tea and I'll see what I can do about my fish." Mack scooped the little stove tin full of water and walked back to the hillside out of the wind and made a rock corner and set up his tiny propane stove. Vonnie stood, her rod against her side and tied on another fly.

The BlackBerry said now: Not east; W slope. Two mile line. Mack smiled. Needle in a two-mile haystack.

Vonnie slowly walked the rocks, small steps, her binoculars at her eyes, and then she stopped. Mack watched her: a motionless figure on a silver plate. She knelt, still looking out where the fish held, and placed the field glasses on the rock shore. She worked her arm back and forth twice and then looped a slow cast that ran out onto the sunny lake surface. Mack's stove hissed; the simmering water had begun to bubble in the two-cup tin.

He heard a crack and the sky echoed it. A rifle shot somewhere below. Vonnie turned, a question mark on her face, and Mack saw her rod start and then bend double.

"Here he is," she said. Mack started to stand but saw that Vonnie wasn't going to be delicate about it this time. She hauled and reeled once, and then, her rod in a horseshoe, she backed away from the lake. The trout slid onto the land, twisting like a dervish, a blur, and still Vonnie backed until he was well away from water. She knelt and secured him and tapped his skull quickly and then again. She lifted the big fish like a bouquet and grabbed her rod and joined Mack in the rocky lee.

"What was that, a shot?"

"Somebody sighting in a rifle."

"Or poachers," she said. "You can't sight in up here. You can't be shooting."

"You're not supposed to. Is that the same fish?" he said.

"Check it," she said, lifting the two-foot brown so Mack could see the two leaders coming from his noble jaw.

Mack smiled. "The same fish twice. I've never seen it."

Out of the wind it was warm and Mack retrieved two paper cups from his daypack and poured the tea. Vonnie sat a minute and then quickly knelt and drew her knife, making the vent cut and the gill cross in each fish and then pulling out the guts in a single pull, expertly, and thumbing out the blood. She walked to the lake and rinsed them and washed her hands.

When she returned with the big browns on a gill cord, she said, "How close was that shot?"

Mack looked up and made a circle with his hand. "Up here, in the valley. A mile, two. Not three."

"Let's see your hands."

She held them out. "What do you see; I'm not nicked up."

"Some ring," he said. She took her hands away and picked up the tea. "You and Kent going to have kids?"

"He doesn't want them. We're not married."

"You're engaged."

"I'm not engaged."

"He gave you a silver ring with those three stones that look a lot to me like diamonds."

"It's a ring."

"Didn't that lawyer get down on a knee and say, 'Yvonne, please marry me'?"

"He gave me a ring."

"I don't feel as if I'm getting full disclosure here, but it's a nice ring. You moved in with him."

"I did."

"That's a big house. Is it called a house?" She sipped her tea and looked out over Spearpoint. "Did you take your books out of that dairy crate?" She looked at him over her tea. For a moment it was as quiet as the sky, quiet as it should have been with all of the world far below them. He said, "You want some sugar cubes? Sugar cubes are very fine when drinking tea in the big mountains. I forgot." He pulled out a paper sleeve and unwrapped the sugar cubes. "Take two. I don't have enough sugar cubes in my own life."

There was a new noise now, a squeal and then another. "What the hell?" They listened. "It sounds like wild turkeys." Then there was a bass whoop and the unmistakable cadence of voices. "Sit still," Mack said.

It was periodic but ascending and two minutes later the clear words could be heard: "See, see, see!" A person climbed into view at the spearpoint, and then another and two more, young people in sweatshirts and hiking shorts. Two girls and two boys.

"See! My god," a female voice said. "What a weird place!" One of the young men lay down flat on his back on the rocks there, and the three others stood with their hands on their knees catching their breath. "Is that snow?"

"What do you want to do?" Mack said.

"Nothing," Vonnie said. "Wait. Hope they turn around. Finish this tea. They won't see us if we don't move."

"No way!" one of the girls cried.

"Way way," the other said, pulling her shirt off. They were throwing their clothing onto the boy on the ground who was lying inert in the laundry.

"Now what do you want to do?" Mack said. "Drink up. We can hide and watch this carnival or we can make ourselves known."

"That was never your way," Vonnie said to him. She slowly lifted her cup to her mouth in two long sips.

"Or we can quietly slip up over this hill and deadhead back."

Now one of the naked girls had picked her way barefoot to the edge and she jumped in the lake and came up sputtering and swearing and scrambling for her footing. "Oh my god! It's ice!"

Mack had packed the stove and gathered his gear.

"One's a redhead, if you want to know," Vonnie said. She had her binoculars on the group. "Or do you need this provocation?" The boy had jumped in now and then the other girl, grabbing him, and one said, "It's not cold like this." The boy on the ground was lying there, his hands behind his head.

"You're all nuts."

"Come on, James. We're swimming."

Mack and Vonnie moved low over the hill, carrying their fish, and descended; they could still hear the voices, distorted and amplified by the water. "That's too bad," Mack said. "You caught a beautiful fish."

"It's okay. These two are giants. We don't want another. What are four college kids doing in the Winds in September? Don't they have class?"

"They're after their merit badges."

She looked down the slope to where the trees began. "Which way is it?"

They descended steeply down rock to rock, their knees working and warming. "Is it easier to climb up than go down?" Vonnie asked.

"I've heard people say it."

"I'm saying it." The forest was thick here, undergrowth, and Mack led them through the brush, holding branches, going wide around the deadfall. The trees grew bigger as they dropped down and the brush more sparse, and the walking became walking as he followed the drainage, ridge to ridge. They walked an hour as the shade gathered. They were out of the wind, but it was cooling, and they moved without talking. They stopped above a meadow full of elk, all cows, the bulls out of sight, and ate an apple.

"You hungry?" he asked her.

"Not really."

"We'll eat these fish tonight, if we find our camp." They rose and walked around and then across a marshy wood through a rockfall, boulders big as rooms, the ground patterned with elk track.

"You know where we are, don't you?" she asked him.

"I do," he said.

"You've got direction in the woods like no one I know," she said. "I've always loved that about you."

"Thank you very much," he said, "but let's go down here first." They stepped carefully down a broad screefall and into a vale of short pines walking among the trees, no trail. They ascended the far side and out into the scrub meadow, the last clumps of lupine and high mountain sage. Mack looked at where the sun now met the mountain and he checked his watch.

"It got late," Vonnie said.

"We didn't have a lunch," Mack said. "I'm sorry."

"We had one of Hagen's bars and tea by the glacier," she told him. "Who gets that?"

The shadows had thickened even as they stood and talked. The angle of light grew fragile; it made him want to hurry. It had always called to him, and now it hurt. You always felt time as a tangible heartbeat in the mountains. The days were short.

On one fishing trip when he was a boy, his father had talked about it, about how when you slept at eleven thousand feet, you were going so much faster than all the folks sleeping way below you back in the village.

"Faster, sir?" Mack had said.

"That's it. We all go around as the earth turns," he said. He circled a finger. "One day, sunrise to sunrise." He went on. "But sunrise to sunrise in that one rotation, we're way up here and we travel a whole lot further."

"How much?"

"That's for calculus to know," his father had said.

Mack lifted his first finger to make a point. "You're smiling."

His father did smile now. "Okay, right you are, but it's still true. Look around, son. You can feel it. Time up here is precious. You with me?"

"Yes, sir. I am."

Now the mountain air felt rare again, the day lapsing. Vonnie put her hands out suddenly in recognition. "I know where we're going," she said. They stopped as they joined the highline game trail, and she knelt and picked up a large rock from a fall there. "Get your rock."

"Right you are," he said. And he picked up a stone as big as a football. They walked up the faint switchback trail, which Mack himself had made for the first time six years before, and they topped a hillock with three ruined ponderosas standing dead. They'd hauled a lot of stones that year.

The grave was as they'd left it, an oval of stones level in the grassy hilltop. The place was run with faded lupine. He could see Vonnie was affected by the spot and she stood with her stone and looked around at the great circle of the world. "Prettiest gravesite on earth," she said. The air lifted her hair. She walked around and fitted her stone into the pile, saying, "Hey Scout," and Mack laid his there too. The old plank he'd cut at home lay in the rocks, weathered. It said: SCOUT. A DOG.

"You want to say something?" she said.

"I'm glad we're here. He was a good dog who loved to fish."

Vonnie sat on the ground and drank some water from her water bottle. "We haven't been up here."

"Three years," he said. "No, four."

"You should get another dog," she said.

"He had trouble not chasing a cast," Mack said.

"I know all about it," Vonnie said. "He could swim." She handed Mack the bottle and he drank. "We're making it quite a trip."

"Well, we brought two more rocks," he said. "Let's go."

"What was that?"

"What."

She pointed: "A deer? No." She laughed. "I thought I saw somebody."

"Hiram," he said.

"I'm tired," she said. "That's all." She stood up.

They left the trail from the gravesite, crossing south off the hill and in half a mile they dropped onto a path and climbed three hundred yards of hard long uphill strides. Here it was very dark, the periphery run with narrow spears of sky. Then the trail veered off level under some pines, and they were standing in their perfect campsite, quiet and waiting above the blue blanket of Valentine Lake in the burnished late day. "That's why I hang a clothesline," he said.

"To welcome you home," she said.

"So I can find the way," he said. "But welcome home."

Vonnie shook her sleeping bag and lay down on it, unlacing her boots. "You want me to cook?"

"No, I'll do it," he said. She lay and watched the sky, and Mack saw her eyes close. The sun was down behind the western slope.

He cut the heads from the trout and they were still too big for the pan, so he left the tails on and stuffed them with lemon wedges and pepper and butter and double-wrapped them in foil and set them aside. He knelt and fingered together a mound of tinder,

moss, and hairy duff and lit it and fed it up, and the fire rose quiet
and straight. When he looked up from his work, the day was gone,
the mountain sky a bowl of glowing grainy dark. He snugged the
fish into the coals burying them carefully by using a forked stick.
Away from the fire it was chilly and he could hear her napping. He
put his hand on her shoulder and she woke without a word, her
eyes a sleepy kindness, and she crawled into her bag and napped
again. Mack made a tour of the perimeter and gathered an armload
of branches, using half now to stoke the fire. He broke and sorted
the rest into piles close at hand. He shook up a water bottle with
powdered lime punch and set it back on the rock shelf.

There you are, he thought. No trucks, no horses, no buildings
big or small, just the fish and the fire and the sleeping woman. He
wanted the math right, but the sleeping woman was not his sleeping woman and he could do things carefully from this night far
into the unseen days, and it would all still seem borrowed.

When the darkness visited him, he tried to look it in the face.
But it was darkness, so much of it opaque. He would have been the
worst witness for the months behind. He'd had a headache or so it
seemed for five years, always scraping by, eking out, scratching,
and the disappointment yawned and wore at him, something he
never honored by calling it a name. He just let it burrow in and
work him, chasing him from job to job. When Vonnie would try
to talk to him, he left the room and got a beer. She suggested he
open the ranch again and that had him into the whiskey. She
stopped, but he didn't.

One night he ran into Weston Canby at the Silver Saddle after
Mack had stood two weeks at a temporary flagman job at the en-
trance to the national park and he was parched and pissed off.

They knew each other because Mack's father had fired Canby years before. Mack had been thirteen or fourteen and Canby had been stealing firewood by unloading his trucks to the bed sill and then driving off with the balance. This was after he'd been asked to show his permit for taking firewood, and he'd fumbled, saying it was lost. Mack's father let it go once and then stopped the truck exiting the gate the next week. Mack was there where he'd thrown a saddle on the fence bar to rig the stirrup.

"You forgot to unload," his father said to Canby.

"Oh shit," Canby said. "I'm sleeping."

"No, you're not. You're fired. You're stealing this deadwood from public lands and then stealing half from me. Let me add that up: two wrongs, Weston. You can't go up and take things that aren't yours. You're making a bad start in business in this county."

Mack had been startled by Canby's coarse insult and he turned to see the man's face burning as he tromped on the accelerator and roared out of the ranch in a blooming train of dust. For some years Mack remembered the look and avoided places in town where he saw Canby's truck.

In the bar Weston Canby pointed at Mack's face and said, "I got you a drink, flagman. I got you two." Mack couldn't work his knees, and he realized with all the workday dirt on the corners of his forehead that he had no position in which to stand, high horse or low horse.

Mack's father, when offered a free drink in such places, would always answer, "No, thank you kindly. But the time and occasion may give me no chance to reciprocate." Mack had no idea what that meant, but he knew, when he threw back the first of Canby's tequila, that he had crossed the line. Canby folded a hundred-dollar bill under Mack's palm and said, "Enough with the sun-drenched state highway work. I've got a special mission for you, my boy." The feel of Canby's hand on his shoulder was like a claw.

And so it began. He fought with Vonnie and thought such fighting was about being a man, insisting on doing it alone, his way, when in fact he was fighting himself and spoiling his house.

A week later he got a call from Canby and he picked up a rusty yellow Chevy Super Sport in Rawlins, certainly full of meth, and drove it to Gillette and a payoff of seven hundred dollars and a bus ticket home.

Vonnie was gone. He stashed the cash in his dictionary and took the next job. He'd been out driving this way for a month, and people had begun to call him for it. The fourth or fifth run he met Canby outside of Cody, and they talked the way they did standing outside a bar toeing the gravel, and Canby said, "I brought the boy a present." He pointed to a brown hatchback parked there in the dark. "Go ahead now and have fun." Canby's throaty laugh.

There was a person in the car, Trisha. She was twenty-five, pretty and ruined, a full-out addict brittle and electric and she ran him for the next three months which astonished him now; he was a marvel of weakness to himself, and now he shook his head over the high mountain campfire. *Hooked up* was her phrase right off. "Now we've hooked up," the term as ugly as he felt about it. "He's done and now it's you. What's your name?"

Again he felt hollow, nothing in there to check him, put a foot down, stand up. And so he saw it was shame and went for it, caving utterly, crazy on the road then with this woman who never slept but quivered in her seat, her eyes half closed, and when she

was awake, she was climbing him as they crossed the state with
cars full and recrossed it, or she was sitting there staring, always
with a tallboy can of beer between her legs. It didn't take two
weeks of such a life to have him drunk, the hole in him unfillable
or so it felt, and he started throwing empties out the window,
reaching for another beer.

Sometimes she'd climb on his lap while he drove and take his
face in her hands and kiss him while he angled and squirmed to
watch the ninety-mile-an-hour highway. Her eyes were too personal to look at, glassy and wrecked, but she could see him, he felt.
She could see in. "Do you know who wins this kissing contest?"
she'd say, going for his mouth again. "Do you? Do you know?"

"You win," he'd say. "You win." And he'd shake her off back
into her own seat where she'd lift her tallboy in a toast. "I know,"
she'd say. "I am the winner in that department."

One night as they sped heedless through the oil fields, the
flickering silhouettes of antelope on the shoulder for the highway
salt and bunch grass there, she woke from being passed out on his
shoulder and she said, "I know you have another girlfriend."

It sucked the air from his throat, but he said back, "You're not
my girlfriend."

She sat up and found another beer. It was always night in Wyoming then. "I don't care. I'm just your hookup," she said and her
voice got tiny. "And this is the end of the world."

He stuffed all the cash in the dictionary but knew as the season continued that even that would be no recompense. He'd lost
himself.

In Cheyenne one night all they had to do was trade one small
U-Haul trailer for another down at the rail yard and hitch it up, a

job for which the hourly pay would have been nineteen dollars and
he was getting five hundred for the risk. When he freed the delivery trailer, it dropped suddenly and pinned the back of his hand to
the oily ground. He recoiled with the adrenaline and was able to
bump it off with his shoulder, the whole trailer. There on his knees
he took the first deep breath in six months and his eyes burned
over with tears. His goddamned hand. He rolled over and sat back
against the side of the trailer, his hand pressed tight in his armpit,
and here came Trisha with a bottle of Wild Turkey swinging by the
neck, medicine. "Oh, baby," she said, kneeling on him, her bones
sharp on the tops of his thighs, and he closed his eyes and saw it.
These were addicts and drug dealers and they couldn't even secure
a trailer. Not one thing was done square. He took a slug from the
bottle and felt it bite, and he pushed Trisha off as gently as he could
and he held his hand up, meaty and swollen, a blue C stamped into
the back. These were drug dealers. There wasn't going to be fresh
oil in the engines or good tires or a tight lug nut or any single
thing done right. This was a *free fall at the shiterie.* His father said
that at times when things ran careless. He said it at the rodeo any-
time there was a problem with anybody's tack or rope. You coil
your rope in a hurry, you won't have a chance.

An hour later in their miserable motel, he watched himself
bandage the hand and it was the same deal, such imprecision. Trisha ran tape in loops around it until he stopped her. She wanted to
go out and so they went, ending up at a biker bar called the Silver
Trail. Mack kept his hand in his jacket and he could feel his heartbeat there as the flights of drinks arrived. Trisha was pissed that
he wouldn't dance and went out and leaped around, purposely
bumping into the big men in their Levi vests. She was drunk, but

she was always drunk, and Mack could see it was going to be one of their all-nighters. He'd stayed up with her plenty, because going to bed was bad. He couldn't lie there and wait for sleep because everything else came up for him and he had been shown he was a coward in those times. But then an hour later in the Silver Trail she was in a kissing contest hauling with some other woman at two or three men at a side table. "Don't your old man care that you're over here on top of me?" one of the men called out. "You've got more tongue than the devil's sister."

Mack held up his hand from across the room. "No problem." He knew that was always a lie, but he repeated it. When Trisha saw his hand up that way, she went crazy. She turned back to the man as if to deepen their kiss and then she swung, raking his face with her nails and screaming. She started flailing her skinny arms, but the man threw her out onto the floor. Mack didn't move, and he knew everything and saw it all at that moment when he didn't stop the man, who got up and kicked Trisha and then walked around to where she had squirmed on the floor and he kicked her again. Mack himself was drunk, but he knew he couldn't carry any of this. He had five hundred dollars folded in his pocket and it felt like poison and he had ruined his hand and he had not helped the girl who never once in the four months he knew her had helped herself. When he stood, he did it so that the man could come and hit him too, but the moment had passed and the bartender's wife had hauled Trisha to a booth and was holding a towel to her mouth. He showed Trisha the wad of cash money and slid it into the front pocket of her jeans, and he was going to say goodbye, but seeing her eyes, he could not say anything.

It was his worst moment.

Ten days later Wes Canby found him outside a steakhouse in Jackson and they had a talk in Canby's black Toyota pickup. "You can't quit," he told Mack.

"Yeah, I can," Mack said. "I do. I quit. I'm no good for it."

Then Canby did something that Mack had been waiting for. He reached and pulled a blue velour from under the seat and unwrapped a pistol. It was a little black automatic of some kind. The gun, as Canby took hold of it, did nothing to him. He opened the door of the vehicle. "A gun," Mack said. "Not much to shoot here, but you can shoot if you want." He was standing on the ground with his back to Canby.

"You did a job on Trisha," the man said.

"I know it." Mack turned. "We both did."

"She's dead."

"She is not." Mack said it without thinking.

"In her cell in Cheyenne."

Mack put his hands on the truck seat and looked up at Canby. "If I see you again," he said, "I will kill you. Daylight, town square, I don't care."

Weston Canby smiled. "You're a waste of time, sonny. You should take a minute and consider how things really work. You're tied to me ten ways."

He gave in to the shadows in his memory and followed them, thinking this moment was worst, no this, and finally knowing it was when he realized that Vonnie had left, found shelter and more with her old friend Kent. Mack stood with his sickening dictionary and it was the worst moment. The truth was that his worst moments made a long string, and when he finally hit the wall drunk in Jackson, he'd come to long enough to find Kent's car and break the windshield with a tire iron, which seemed a lot more work than it should have been and gave Mack the thought right in the middle of it, *I'm out of shape here, mister—breathing like a lumberjack while I break a glass window?* He was a ruin and when taken to jail, he had vomited in the tank all night, the dry spasms finally cramping his back, feeling in the aftermath a bruise warm like the hand of his lost father. Mack lay in the foul dark place and his hands were scarred and grimy, the cuticles bloody and the scratches a black scribble.

Night came in purple layers. Mack had walked out to the promontory over the black lake so he could look back at the campsite, the tent, the little fire, the spot of his dishtowel. He tried for a star but knew they would only come out all at once and when he looked away. Above a dark lake at night in such a place, it is hard not to think of all the thousand years before and those to come a thousand thousand, regardless of your troubles. Is that it? he thought. Is that what this place does for me?

The fire was a pulsing mound of coals now and Mack fed it up again for the light.

He buttered two slices of pita bread in the frying pan and warmed them.

"I'm cooking here," he whispered.

Her face appeared and she said, "Perfect."

"Are you cold?"

"Not really." She came by the fire and sat on the flat stone. "I fell asleep."

"You want some wine?"

"No, I'm a little dizzy already and I've got the headache."

"Drink this," he said, handing her the green punch.

"Bug juice," she said. "A cure-all."

Mack tugged the foil-wrapped fish from the fire and opened each package gingerly on paper plates. The fish fell apart under their fingers bite by bite and they ate the burned bread and drank the whole quart and then another of the green-flavored punch.

"Were there rocks in the Garden of Eden?" he asked.

"Is that where we were?" They were pinching the trout in the dark and eating it.

"Did that girl really have red hair?"

"She did. A big girl with red hair."

"That's enough information. I'm tired."

"I ate that fish," she said, lifting the skeleton up over the fire and dropping it there.

The night was still and clear and the stars had now all appeared and tripled. They seemed to be stepping closer. "Clear and cold," he said. "You want in the tent?"

"I'm good," she said. She set her paper plate and its tangle of remaining fishbones in the yellow fire and their faces were lit again. "But I'm all in."

"We'll have bear claws for breakfast."

"And your coffee." Vonnie got into her sleeping bag and he saw her squirm out of her clothes and her face disappeared. He burned his plate and caught the ashes.

The screen of the BlackBerry said: Logan Peak E or N. Check. He typed back: Will do am. And then he crawled into the old tent.

Hours later he felt her, the sleeping bag first and then her in it, bumping him knees and back.

"Who is it?" he said. Then he said, "You okay?"

"Yes, it's just cold."

"Oh my, you came into the tent," he said.

"Nothing," she said. "Shut up. Kent knows me."

"He's lucky," Mack said. "Did you wipe your feet?" She shifted and settled against his back and was quiet. "You want me to tell you a story?"

"The cannibal story?"

"No. He wasn't a cannibal. He ate baked fish and bear claws and was very lonely. He was looking for something."

Vonnie was quiet.

"Is that your heart or footsteps?"

"Mack."

"Listen."

"No story," she said.

"He lived in these same woods," he said. "As sad and wrong as you get to be."

"You listen, you shit. He wants *you*. Those are his footsteps coming for *you*."

Then her breath was the breath of the sleeping, and he moved back so she was there, and he closed his eyes and started to say a prayer that also became sleep.

Day Four

Dawn wouldn't come and finally Mack crawled out and saw why: the sky was a solid bank of cover, the gray clouds stuffed tight wall to wall. They'd been loading the sky all night. Because of the overcast the early day was warm and he walked out in his boxers and his unlaced boots to pee. There was no frost and he could smell the pines and the lake. He would check Yarnell's reading when they were up at Clark. It was his last full day with Vonnie and it was at him, his heart, the way he knew it would be. He'd had a bad ten months and now he was better. He could almost accept it; he could get through a day. He went back and knelt, working his tinder fire.

"Get dressed," Vonnie said from her sleeping bag in the tent.

"I'm starting the fire," he said. "You want to eat, no?"

"Put your pants on."

He pulled his clothing from the tent and looked at her. "You warm enough?"

"Perfect," she said. "Thanks for the shelter."

Seeing her in the old tent in the gray day required him to turn and open the cooking kit. He'd been surprised about how all of it operated in his body, sharp moments everywhere, primarily in his stomach, but also his upper back and forehead. He'd cried most of a month and that place was still weak. Mack built the fire up into a smokeless orange torch, two feet, and let it shrink so he could place the wire rack over it on the rocks. He set the coffeepot on the grill and a pan of water and when the black frying pan was warm, and the butter started to wander, he laid in the two golden bear claws and cracked his six eggs around them.

"You're cooking," she said. He took the warm water over to her in the tent and handed her the clean dishtowel. She sat up in her sleeping bag and covered her lap with the bundle of her jacket and jeans and she washed her face in the gray morning. "I'm stiff," she said. "Aren't you?"

"Gimme," he said, drawing her blue wool shirt from her hands and holding it before the fire, front and back and front again. When the inside was warm he took it to her and she put it on.

"Thank you, sir," she said. "That's nice."

"We can stop at Mowram's tomorrow on the way to town," he said.

"They're closed."

"I'll call him."

"I'm not getting in a hot pool with you."

"Vonnie, you can trust me. Look, you're in my tent."

"Mack, I came up here. And I'm glad I did. I trust you. I guess. But this trip is it. You know that." She rubbed her ears hard and handed him the towel and smiled, all clean. "I'll see you in town."

He said, "From time to time. Maybe at the post office. I'll carry your packages."

"No you won't."

"This mess is ready," he said, showing her the fry pan. "Let's eat."

She dressed and came out into the dark day. "Rain," she said. He doubled the paper plates and handed her one with a fork. "One stop shopping," she said, looking at the pastry and eggs. "I'm not set up for rain, but maybe it will hold off."

"Maybe it will snow," he said. "We'll have to camp in, have you trust me all winter."

The sky was a gray pillowed gridlock. They ate the eggs and tore the warm bear claws into sections which they dunked in the strong milky coffee. Mack wiped out his pans and handed Vonnie his plates. "Here, you do the dishes." She slid the egg-smeared paper plates into the fire. He stood up and looked out over the sullen sheet of Valentine Lake. "Well," he said. "Let's get ourselves up to Clark and close this party down."

They packed daypacks and rejoined the main trail, walking a mile and a half to the wooden bridge over the Wind in the long meadow. Sitting on the logs, they shook out their boots and retied them. "Oh my," Mack said. He pointed to a thick line of white smoke above them in the river valley, rising and knotted and turgid in the overcast. "The undergraduates are having a big breakfast."

"They need a lesson from you in campfires."

He stood. "Let's go around. We can go up to Lower Divide Lake and over from there." The smoke drifted now along a distinct ceiling through the mountain valley. They turned and followed the main trail east past the Forest Service sign for Little Joseph Lake and on to the unmarked foot trail to Upper Divide. This side of the mountain cirque was open, tall brush, grass and willows ascending through a broad marshy drainage. There were plank and log bridges in the low places and in the warm close day they could smell the sweet marsh grass and pine. It felt good again

to walk and they didn't talk. About halfway up Vonnie stopped
him with her open hand on his chest. He'd been watching his feet
and he looked up to see the moose, a cow right next to the trail. She
lifted her head and looked over her shoulder at them, chewing. Her
coat was lush this late in the season, deep brown, and her eyes
were calm. She chewed and held the stare. After a full minute Vonnie pushed him back and they retreated to a place where they could
go up and around. They didn't speak even regaining the trail on
the other side of the meadow, climbing now through the switchbacks on the last hill below the lake.

"A lot of detours on a day," she said.

Upper Divide was a ten-acre lake lined on the upper side by
the rock slope. Mack and Vonnie followed the overgrown trail
along the lake's edge to where the trees gave onto the talus. She
sat on a block of granite and pulled out her canteen. Mack sat.

"Our moose," he said. They had camped here one year, across
the lake in a place that had a huge log fallen across which had
been all furniture to them, table, shelf, chair. They'd made love
against it. "I know where your initials are right over there," Mack
said now.

"It's not our moose," Vonnie said, handing him the water.
"You're just full of ghosts."

"I've got a living memory, if that's what you mean."

"You're like a bus full of ghosts."

"Perhaps," he said. "Yeah, there are ghosts. You don't have
any?"

"No, sir," she said.

"Not even me?"

"No, Mack, not even you."

"That is one hell of a therapist you've got."

"It's dark as night," she said. "I could use some sun."

"Not today, I'm afraid." She was already up and on the trail where it crossed away from the lake on its way up to Clark. Now the walking was level, traversing the mountainside in the tall trees, a quiet, humid twilight, and they breathed and talked as she led him five feet ahead along the way.

"What are your plans? And don't make something up."

"I'm going to get on top of my debts, save the ranch, most of it."

"What was it, chapter seven?"

"I'm not talking about this."

"Kent knows. Come on, Mack."

"Kent knows all about it; he represents half my creditors. Chapter seven, eight, nine, ten, eleven and what have you. I'll be good for every dollar, just not this year."

"What's that?" Vonnie said, lifting her head, smelling something. They stood as if listening and Mack could smell the powerful odor of loam.

"Dirt?" he said. They filed around a narrow corner formed by a rock palisade and were confronted by a fresh talus slide, the dirt and rocks rolled into a mound the size of three houses, fanning downhill. They stepped back and assessed the phenomenon.

"Wow," Vonnie said. She looked at the rock pile.

"Let's go down around," he said.

"You lead," she said. "When did this happen?"

"Probably last spring when it froze and thawed three times." The huge spillage was a regular landslide and the leading edge abutted two great folds of torn earth and twisted trees, cockeyed and still growing at desperate angles. Grasses and tiny wildflowers were sprouting at the seams. They followed the far side up again under the mountain shoulder and into the tall trees which grew taller and then even more majestic as they walked. There was already a new trail around the obstruction, oddly well worn for a game trail. It dipped and followed up to the original path they'd been on and they continued into big timber. Here the trees were truly grand, twenty feet apart with trunks four feet in diameter and branches that started thirty feet from the ground. There was no undergrowth at all, just duff and packed earth in the dark place and it was quiet.

"This is weird here," she said.

"Magical," he said. They both saw it for what it was, the kind of grove where they would have stopped and made love in the old days. The privacy was overwhelming, a feeling in his chest. "Do you want me to tell you a story?"

"The cannibal was scrupulous and full of regret, but no story," she said, "thanks." Now there was the sound of a stream, but they came to none. The temperature dropped a little in the glade.

"What is that?" she said.

Mack stopped and said, "It's raining."

Now it could faintly be felt, the mist pooling from the interwoven canopy. The feeling of enclosure was complete; they walked on in silence through the forest rooms.

"I love this," Vonnie said.

"These are the oldest trees up here." They continued another hundred yards when Mack stopped short and, back against a tree, grabbed Vonnie's arm and drew her to him.

"Don't."

"Quiet." His serious face made her stop struggling.

"What is it?" She knew to whisper.

"There," he tipped his head. "Look there." Across the dark space made by the mossy trunks was a gray tent. It all came into focus: the fire ring and the big tent, and two gutted elk hanging by the heels from a horizontal log nailed to two of the big trees. He watched her face and whispered, "Anybody?" They were both still.

She looked over his shoulder. "No."

"Smoke in the fire?"

"No." She stood against him.

"Shit," he said.

"Poachers." She reached into her front pocket and withdrew a tiny camera and stepped to take a picture.

Mack had been jolted. The stark tableau was obscene in the dim forest enclave and had thrown over the day. There was blood on the trees. "Let's go, Vonnie."

"These assholes."

He could hear the camera firing. "Enough, go back." They turned and walked quickly up the way they had come, hurrying. As they proceeded, there was less cover and the rain now fell steadily, not a passing rain. At the rock slide they sat under a tree and broke out the canteens.

"Nice camera," Mack said. "Kent give you that too?"

"Do you know where we are?" she asked him.

"Yes, I could report it."

"Okay then."

"You got your phone in your car."

"In my pocket."

"You had your phone?"

"Don't act surprised. Kent told me to."

"So much for our agreement," he said. He heard the device chime as it powered up. Vonnie watched the screen. "No service."

"We're against this hill," he said. "Let's go up to Clark and you can make your phone calls."

"Mack, we're going back. We want away from these guys."

He knew she was right; it was bad business in the woods. They looked real. This wasn't a story; these were guys set up for butchering; there'd been other elk hanging here all summer. "Okay, let's go."

As he spoke, a figure came up from the torn earth out of the crazy tilted trees and behind him another man. It was everything Mack did not want to see; it was like watching an accident. They were carrying a twelve-foot pole on which was tethered a gutted cow elk, her head hanging and grazing the trail as they approached. Mack stood as the first man saw him, and then Vonnie stood. The man wore dirty khakis and a long-sleeve black T-shirt with a shooting vest over it. His rifle was shouldered with a strap. He was about forty and his expensive haircut was parted on one side. He didn't stop but stared at the two, Mack and then Vonnie, walking closer. The second man was older and heavier, all in denim shirt and pants. This guy was chewing something rapidly and his eyes were glassed. His scoped rifle was shouldered as well and he had a homemade buzz haircut that was a week old.

Mack measured it all and took Vonnie's hand and pulled her up behind him. "Howdy," Mack said.

Neither of the men answered. The two men just looked, and

then the first man, the younger one who had an actor's narrow face, said, "Hello, Mack."

Vonnie gasped.

"Canby," Mack said.

They both looked at the elk tied to the pole.

"What the hell?" the heavy man said. His shirttails were out and there was blood on both thighs of his pants. He was the one with the big knife, Mack guessed. His face looked caught, scared.

"Such luck," Wes Canby said. "You dumb fuck." He shifted his load and smiled. "You going to kill me?"

"We're fishing," Mack said. "Just fishing."

"Not anymore," Canby said. The rain fell and sounded over them all. The two hefted their dead weight and the elk's head bobbed below its slit throat.

"We didn't see you," Mack said. He pulled Vonnie past the first man, and past the elk steaming in the rain, ripe and gamy, and past the bloody man.

"Put it down," Canby said to his partner, and they began to lift their burden to the side.

"Go," Mack said, pushing Vonnie ahead of him on the trail. "Run." She did. Two steps, and she was striding nicely through the wet track. Mack followed, and the first twenty steps he made sure he stayed between her and the poachers. He could feel the shot coming, and then they were down and around a turn, and then fifty yards and a hundred. The rain had dropped a notch and settled in for the long haul everywhere. It felt oddly warm. He hated running in the woods. Vonnie was sprinting and Mack fought to catch her daypack and pull her back.

"Just jog, watch your step. Don't race and don't fall." The trail was wet and then became a stream, and they ran splashing along the mountain trail as it rose and dipped against the high slope. They ran and he waited for the adrenaline to subside and for his knees to burn, but it did not subside and they ran on. He hadn't looked at his watch and he hated that too. He didn't know how long they'd been running. The mud gathered in the cleats of their boots and all of their footprints were magnified; easy to see. It would be like following an elephant. They ran through the grass where they could, but always they had to return to the muddy furrow. His heart was hammering flint and then it too settled into a drum and he got his vision back and they dropped down the trail. They could not outrun a 30.06 or a 273. They couldn't outrun a .22 squirrel gun. They ran out of the forest and through a meadow, willow green in the muted day, and then into the trees again where the footing was a touch more secure, the wet dirt without the grasses. Vonnie had always been a good runner; they'd done two ten-K's when? Seven years ago, six? She made you want to run, because she was so fluid and it looked easy. When Mack ran it looked like work. She glided now five yards ahead of him, slowing sometimes to make sure of the trail, and twice they had to stop and back up to find it. Every time they came into the small meadows the rain seemed to have increased. They broke into a narrow meadow that Mack didn't recognize and Vonnie slipped, clutched at a willow, and went down on her back, striking her thigh on the rocks. She hopped immediately up and fell down again.

"Oh shit, Mack." Her cargo shorts were soaked and the wound was there on her thigh, a five-inch gash clawed by the stones and already printed with blue bursts. It looked angry and embedded with dirt. He fingered a small stone from her flesh and she gasped. "No no," she whispered. "Don't touch."

There was no time to assess it. He pulled her backward, hands under her arms off the trail twenty feet, regretting the bent grass. Her eyes were open and she wasn't pale. They were breathing heavily and still he left her there and he circled up and regained the trail and then ran along another fifty yards, making a big show there of turning into the upside woods. He stood a moment and then threw his fishing pole down, the coup de grâce. He couldn't remember the last false trail he'd laid; it would have been in a game as a kid. In the duff he could walk without marking and he again circled and found Vonnic. Now she was truly pale and her eyes were saucered.

"I'm okay."

"We're ditching," Mack said. He pointed. "We'll go down deadhead and hide."

He stood her up, and she fell over his shoulder in a fireman's carry, and she said, "Oh," quietly, but he felt her clench against the pain. Mack stepped heavily down through the branched deadfall and willows in a slow serpentine trying to keep from falling. Their breathing was synchronized now and they chuffed with each step. Two hundred yards farther and he was in the marsh, ankle deep which he hated, but every step allowed the willows to close behind them which he loved. He'd spent a lifetime taking the highline trails and now he was in the real muck. He continued swinging his steps down, trying to find anything elevated, some firm grace, but every weedy tuft turned out to be the same silt. He was glad he'd tied his boots so well. He was sweating in the rain and he marched left-foot-right until the adrenaline was off him, though he didn't know if it had been a half hour or an hour. "I'm okay," Vonnie would whisper from time to time into his back. "I hurt my leg is all." Blinded by sweat, he stepped off the grassy bank into a beaver pool and went to his crotch in the water.

"Christ."

He stopped and heard Vonnie say, "Water." He located the dam, the mounded pile of sticks the size of a car and he waded slowly over to it.

"I'm going to set you here," he told her.

"Oh," she said. And with her heavily in his shoulder and tightly in his hands, he stepped up and leaned slowly forward until he was afraid he'd drop her and then he felt her bottom find the dam, and she held him now against her there as her face slid down along and past his own. "You can move your hands, mister. Thanking you very much," she said. Her eyes were hooded and she boosted herself up out of the pond, her stunned face up in the rain, a tight-lipped grimace on her face.

"Okay a minute?"

"Okay a minute," she said back to him.

Mack pushed around the pond, ten yards through the water now to his waist, and crawled out on all fours across the clearing from Vonnie. She smiled at him now and said, "It's not bad," but the corners of her mouth were tucked and trembling. Her beauty was a light in his chest, the delicacy of her face. He stood as best he could and stepped away into the marsh again looking for high ground and shelter. He crossed an acre of spongy grass and then mounted into the forest once more. It wasn't dry ground but it was ground. He kicked his boots against a tree to free the mud, and he put his hands on his knees and tried to still himself and think of the next thing, but his thoughts would not line up. He had to get her. Mack stepped back into the swale and then the open pond and across to Vonnie who held her face down in the rain. She seemed now to be nodding at him for some reason, at everything.

"Are you okay? Can you hear me? Are you cold? I found a place we can hide." He couldn't lift her from where he stood, and so she turned and he put his hands under her arms. He could only drag her, her heels bumping and gliding through the wet place. Under the sketchy shelter of the pines, he examined the wound, careful not to press. It was a radical contusion but he didn't think anything was broken. Her entire leg was covered with watery blood, but the bleeding had generally stopped and the rim of the cut was blue now and gray. Mack gathered a small bundle of kitchen match kindling, breaking the wiry leads from the underbrush, two handfuls, and he gave them to Vonnie and said, "Put this under your shirt against your belly." She did. He gathered fifty finger sticks, all wet, and set them against a tree trunk. He gathered twenty branches, careful not to snap them, and laid them by the others in a loose stack which if the rain abated half would allow them to dry. He put his hand on Vonnie's forehead.

"I fell, quite heavily, on my ass," she said. "But I can tell you who is the vice president." It was the question you asked concussion victims when they opened their eyes, an old joke of his father's, because of a kid who fell off a horse when Gerald Ford was president.

"You want some tea," he asked her.

"Oh my god," she said. "That would be nice. With those sugar cubes, thank you." She was whispering. "I've become dedicated to your sugar cubes."

He assembled his stove under the tree and scooped and rescooped a tin of water from the rivulet above the beaver dam.

"We can have a fire after dark," he told her.

"This is a bivouac," she said.

"It is."

"Is it dark yet? I'm kidding. But I'm going to want a hot stone," she said. She was testing her wound with her fingers, pressing each side and making faces.

"Next you'll try to get up," he said. "Don't do that. We can try for that in the morning."

"That is a great stove," she said. "I'm a dedicated fan of your stove and those sugar cubes."

Mack watched her face and couldn't read it. He told himself to stop worrying, because worry only made decisions into wet knots, his father said. He needed simple assessment. *You did this,* he thought. *This is you, all the way.* Vonnie sat sideways on her good leg, against a wet tree. She was pale but she could talk. They had the tea with sugar cubes and an apple which he sliced and the day lunch he'd brought of pita bread and cheese, and he boiled some more water and they had weaker tea with twice as much sugar. She took some aspirin. The rain was an unwavering fact, but under the tree they dried as fast as they got wet and it continued. The dark came in vertiginous increments; it took hours. It had been so dark all day, the evening was imperceptible. After seven Mack stood and went to the edge of the trees and saw finally that the light had drained.

"I've got to pee," Vonnie said.

"Let's try the standing thing."

She lifted her arms and said, "Wait, my shirt is full of sticks." Mack took them and stuffed them now dry into his daypack. He stood before her with her hands in his and her feet braced against his boots. He pulled her up and she stood. In the gloom he saw the wave of faintness cross her face and pass.

"Here," she said, adjusting him on her injured side.

"We won't go far." With her arm over his shoulder they made ten steps, three trees.

"Now what?" she said. "Oh hell, Mack, hum something."

"What?"

"That annoying hobo song." She had him turn face away.

"Here's to you, my rambling boy," he sang softly. *"May all your rambling bring you joy. Late one night in a jungle camp, the weather it was cold and damp, he got the chills and he got them bad. I lost the only friend I had. Then here's to you, my rambling boy, may all your ramblings bring you joy. That's all I know."*

"That's not enough for this trip," she said from below. "Sing it again." He did, and then she pulled herself up.

"Thank you, sir."

"I'll learn the whole song for next time."

"Do that."

He built a fire the size of his hand, keeping all his fuel nearby. The first white finger of smoke was hope itself; the fire worked and wavered in the rain but not enough to worry him. Their poachers had their own fire to worry about. Mack gathered his dry sticks. He lay on his side and had Vonnie lie between him and the fire—on her good side.

"You okay?"

"I'm okay," she said. "I paid a price for running in the woods, Mack, but I'm okay." A minute later she said, "No service."

"Turn it off and save that battery," he said. "Kent would want you to." He laid his arm out for her head and his other arm he put across her belly from where he would feed the small wood into the fire.

"That was the guy you worked for?"

"Canby. He's a dealer and he's smart, knows everybody. I saw him tie good knots when he was loaded." Mack felt his air go out and now he whispered. "I drove for him and did the rest."

She was quiet and then in a small voice she said, "Did you love that girl?"

"I was with that girl. I was. I was as crazy as you get to be and now sorry the same way, but I know what love is, Vonnie, and the answer is no. If it was yes, I would say yes."

"Did she love you? Trisha?"

"No one knows that, not even her. She had a wild way of talking, but she never said *love*, and I never saw her when she wasn't impaired or headed hard for it."

"How could you."

The water moved everywhere, draining and dripping, merging with the sound of the light touches of wind, and Mack fed the small fire. "I don't know, Vonnie." He sorted a handful of little sticks, piece by piece. "Vonnie. She died. I heard and then saw it in the papers. She never came back from being out there. Part of it is on me."

"I wondered. I knew about it. I'm sorry, Mack."

"I am, my friend. I'm sorry."

After a moment, Vonnie said, "Bivouac."

"Just like uptown," he said.

"I'm going to need a story," she said. "What was his name?"

"His name was Hiram Corazon."

"Was he Mexican?" she asked.

"He was Canadian," Mack said, "but from a province that no longer exists. The two rivers thawed and the province disappeared."

"It was small," she said.

"Big enough for the village."

"Where he met the girl," Vonnie said. "And her name was."

"Lucinda Amateur."

"It was a dear family."

"It was," he said. "Full of Amateurs. They farmed goose down and made comforters for the town."

"Oh my, a thick goose-down comforter."

"Five inches thick."

"And dry."

"Absolutely."

"How did they meet?" Vonnie said. "No, how did he lose her?"

"Which?" They were whispering.

"Meet," she said.

"They met the same way he lost her." Mack spoke from the edge of his own sleep.

"Tell me."

"It was because of the lost goose."

"I don't know this part. This is the cannibal, right?"

"Vonnie, listen. People thought he was a cannibal and he got that reputation of a cannibal and the legend needed a cannibal, but what Hiram Corazon did was something very tender and surprising."

Vonnie shifted back against him. "Are you cold?"

"Yes," he said. "It's how I know we're here."

"I'm okay. It's a good little fire we have here."

He could feel her face on his arm. "Okay," he said. Mack felt it in his gut, the worry, but talking could keep it off him. He thought about the airplane part, Yarnell's mission, and the stupid money. He wanted it still. The next bad choice. The woods now were dark dripping curtains, but the fire held against them, and Mack spoke into Vonnie's hair. He spoke slowly as the words appeared for him.

"They were young and wanted to help their families in the village and they took work collecting down at the goose station. Geese stopped at the station going north in the summer and going south in the winter. They could eat corn at the station and talk and spend two or three days resting and reading. Putting their webbed feet up. Geese have big feet that they like to rest at any chance. In the winter Hiram curried the southbound ducks, harvesting the down. They loved it. Many of the geese got facials as well and their beaks polished, *beakicures.*" That Vonnie didn't ask about that word told him she was asleep, but he was almost asleep and kept whispering. "Big bales of down for the village comforter factory, the finest down comforters in all the Americas and parts of Manchuria, where they had an outlet. One day at the end of work Hiram discovered one of the southbound geese missing, and he was responsible for every goose. He knew this goose, whose name was Robert Guatemala, because he was the mayor of a flock that wintered in that country, was not scheduled to depart until

the morning. He consulted with his down-currying associate Lucinda Amateur about what to do. They had closed the grooming
shop and put their tools away the way they had done for a year.
He loved the way she put the tools away, and he loved the way she
curried the down and treated the southbound geese, and Hiram
Corazon knew that he loved Lucinda Amateur, but he did not
know what to do about it. He was going to tell her every next day,
and he never told her. He lived his life at the edge of telling her.
When she was near him his heart was beating. He could hear it
beating even when the geese called. Lucinda said, we need to find
that goose, even one goose; we must find him. So they went out
into the northern night of the lost province and began searching.
There were only two places to look. East of the village and west of
the village." Mack repeated that sentence and then said *village*
one more time seeing the girl go into the dark and then he was
asleep.

Day Five

It was a cold camp in the dripping dawn. Mack opened his eyes in the new light, and he could see through the pines that the sky was a sharp torn blue and the broken clouds were wispy and dissipating as the sun came. The cold had been working against his back for hours, not the thievery of a wind but the ever-moving air that left him with cramping chills. Rays of sunlight fell through the forest in slanted columns, catching the great branched spiderwebs here and there; the effect was churchlike, and Mack thought that, but he was cold now, deeply, and his back hurt. He held Vonnie firmly in his arm, her back curled to his front down to their crossed ankles. Everything was damp even their small bowl of ashes in the ground, and they could have no fire. He was cold and he knew that moving would make him colder. There was no heat in the planks of sunlight. He sat up.

"What?" Vonnie said. "Are you cold?" She folded herself tighter.

"Hold still, I want to look at your leg." The wound was swollen and now stains of blue had come up on every side, but it was not red or infected. He was on his hands and knees above her and looked into her face, her hair collapsed into a cone around it. She gave him the *who me* smile and said, "Can I walk? Will I dance again? Really what I want to know is, will I be warm again?" She lifted her hands and he took them. "Help me." It was a life of this, the two of them, all hands joined, about to do the next thing.

"Love to," he said. "Hello, Vonnie."

They paused like that a moment and she met his face and said,

"Hello, Mack," and then she nodded and he pulled her up. She grimaced and stood. "Rub my back, Mack, will you. Send those chills to China."

He braced her with his forearm across her clavicle and kneaded his knuckles up and down her back. She shivered and then let go and came into his embrace, and he heard her catch a sob. Her hand clenched on his shirtsleeve, and then she straightened. "Okay," she said, "it's cold. What are we doing?" She had her phone out again. "No service here."

"Try it," he said, pointing at her leg.

"It's got to work," she said. "We're not staying here. This was a fine place, but we used it up."

"Okay then," he said, "let's go to Valentine." She rolled her hips left and right and lifted each knee.

"Can't run," she said, "but let's march." She leaned forward and commenced an irregular stride. Mack sighted and started walking west, down through the soaking brush that had them both wet again in a minute. He bushwacked in a long arc finally intersecting the Upper Divide trail well below where they dropped it yesterday. There were no tracks in the muddy trail, but Mack moved slowly and looked up and down. They were both shivering. He stopped and found Vonnie a patch of dry ground in the sunlight.

"Wait here a second," he told Vonnie. "I'm going up to see something." He helped her sit. Mack climbed by walking aside the trail in the bunch grass trying to leave no tracks. A quarter mile above his pole was where he had thrown it by the trail and there were no tracks at all. Canby and his buddy hadn't even come this far. He opened the BlackBerry and there was a flashing blue light.

What the hell. He couldn't get the screen to go on, but the blue dot pulsed in the corner every second.

When he rejoined Vonnie, she saw his fishing pole and said, "Good. They didn't follow."

"Not on this trail."

"Is there one above?"

"Above and below. Let's go." Vonnie found her leg warmed to the walking; it was better when she was moving.

"How long have they been operating?" she said to Mack.

"All summer from the looks of it."

" 'We're just fishing,' you told them."

"That was lame." He immediately added, "Excuse my language. It was poor. I couldn't come up with anything else. I have no recollection of what I said."

"You're a horrid liar."

"I am. That's why I gave it up."

"You sure said, 'Go.' "

"It's worked for me in the past. Oh hell, Vonnie." He took her elbow, stopping close in the woods. "I should have told them that this was our last trip and I wanted them not to wreck it in any way and I wanted them to stop poaching elk and find meaningful work. Like I'm going to do." Mack was surprised he could joke.

Vonnie, limping, led them down to the main valley trail and then to the wooden bridge crossing of the Wind. The sun was out and warmer, but the light had changed, tilted and it felt so much later in the year than it had two days before.

"Do you need to stop?"

"No, let's have some water and go up to camp and get dry socks and get absolutely out of here." Mack didn't like being in the open meadow, but any other route would have cost them an hour and kept them wet. They crossed the river and climbed out of the open space into the forest, slow and steady now and warmed by their efforts. "You knew the other guy?" she asked.

"I may have seen him, but I don't know. I may have seen him in the paper for that big meth farm down in Rawlins and such. I think I met him a time when I was loaded. I don't know; he may have been the cook. Christ, I may have been working for him." Reaching into the dark like this spent Mack and braced him; he had done things of which he had only shadowy recall. It took his breath.

"How'd you stop drinking?" she said.

"Suddenly and permanently," Mack told her. "I don't joke about it."

"Those weren't new rifles."

"No, they weren't, but we're in their thoughts this morning, dear, and it's the kind of thinking I don't care for." They climbed the last steps on the narrow trail and turned above Valentine Lake.

Their camp was trashed. The place was tilted wrong and took a moment to settle in their vision. Trashed. The sight was a mess of boot prints and the cooking kit had been kicked around and into the rocks and brush. The tent was gone and their packs. Vonnie took Mack's arm and backed him up before they entered the area. They turned and walked down a hundred paces and he stopped her and nodded left. She followed up, wending through the pines and sandstone until they emerged along the bluff above the site. Mack scanned the sky. "I'd like to see those kids' camp smoke about now." They knelt in the sunlight and waited twenty minutes not talking. Valentine Lake changed beneath them from a thin sky blue to flat gray and then under the sun it went green. They stood and walked into camp.

"They left the clothesline," Mack said. He was gathering the pans and cups and forks and he found the goody bag of cheese and crackers and candy.

"There," Vonnie said, pointing down. The two sleeping bags were snagged on the rocks and he could see his tent in the lake six feet under on a rock shelf.

"I've got my knife and matches," he said.

"Where are your car keys?"

"On the passenger rear tire. Like always," he said.

"Same as mine. I've got my knife."

"And those flies," he said.

She had taken off the fishing vest and draped it on a little pine to dry. "We've got to go," she said. "You want to grab the sleeping bags?"

"I don't know," he said. "I'm a little confused." He sat down on the warm rock and held his head. He could feel the friction there, the fatigue.

"You look weird," she said.

"You look weird," he said. But he said it quietly without looking. Now he lay back with his heavy arm over his eyes.

"You're soaked," she said.

"You're soaked," he said. Vonnie climbed down to the lake by sitting on each rock step. She dragged one of the sleeping bags up and stood above him.

"We can't stay here," he said.

"Then come on, mister. Let's go up beside the lake out of sight.

They won't come back and if they do, they won't see us. We'll leave the stuff, the tent and the one bag. Bring that food. Leave the pans." She kicked his foot. "Come along." She pointed at him. "Leave your dear clothesline and come along."

They found a place two hundred yards farther, an open room in the rocks, and in the sunlight Vonnie unzipped the sleeping bag and spread it on the dry duff. "Yeah," she said. "You look funny. You're blue."

"You're blue," he said.

"I've got a cramp in my back."

"It's the cold from last night," he said. But he could feel the pressure in his head, the fever, waving across, working now steadily behind his eyes.

"Give me those wet pants," she said. She sat and took off her boots, unlacing them and opening them on the sunny sandstone and then she did the same with his boots and sopping socks, hanging them on a branch.

"That's better," he said, and then she pulled his Levi cuffs until he squirmed out of the wet heavy garment, his legs gooseflesh.

"Get in," she said, and he rolled into the sleeping bag and she covered him over and zipped the bag. "Give me that shirt and your underwear." His eyes were already closed, but he complied. "You want an apple," she said, taking a bite and chewing. She sat against a log, her legs stretched out in the thin sunlight.

"No," he said.

"You want a story?" she said, but his answer was sleep.

————

Nothing he had done made money. The bookstore was ridiculous; they did better on greeting cards and then that just petered out and he closed the rented storefront and hauled boxes of books to the Western Horizons rest home south of town, and then his computer consulting kicked in, or he tried to jump-start it, and it looked like it would really go until his start-up expenses told the truth. Then it was month to month and the mortgage went untended. He liked the computer work some of the time, but only some. He wanted the ranch with all his heart, and he knew he needed to gather his gumption and run the guest ranch again. He didn't want to raise livestock of any stripe. He could farm, but not really very well. He'd prefer to repair equipment all winter and had done so, rather than drive any of the tractors even a week in the good weather. There were times when he felt stupid, a fraud, some guy with a soft heart for the ranch and no real reason. Finally he decided he didn't care what it was, but it was that he wanted the place where he'd grown up. He saw the town change and change again and it would never ever stop; there would be curbs and gutters clear to Dubois. But home is home, he told himself, and worth fighting for. When Yarnell showed up, he was about to start his EMT and join the county ambulance squad; trouble was up and harm and general injury, and he'd been part of it, the carelessness, but he had gathered enough of himself to know that he was good in hot moments. If he'd been able to keep Vonnie, these would be good days.

He woke in a dry bake, wonderful, face down, drooling a little onto the deep green liner of Vonnie's sleeping bag. There was a distant crack, the rifle, and a second later the ruined hollow echo broke against the mountain. He swallowed and turned over on his back, his arches taking a stretch he hadn't planned. The sun was a silver star in his eyes. His head hummed now fainter. Sometimes being warm was just the cure. He sat up and was alone with the quick air on his bare chest, the sky now a solid serious winter blue.

"Vonnie," he said. Across Valentine Lake the mountain had given up its last morning shadow and stood like a great amphitheater, a million gray seats, the ghosted shushing descending the cascade. It was grand here, larger than a person could understand, except to be challenged by it, made real and temporal and quiet and humble the way a prayer sometimes worked near the heart, not always but sometimes. The vault of air between the man and the mountain called to Mack, but he couldn't tell to what, the old feeling that something was going to happen next. "Vonnie," he said again.

His blue chambray shirt was on the rock, dry where the sun hit it, and his underwear. Standing up he found his socks and boots. He walked to the perimeter of the sunny rock circle. Vonnie sat cross-legged out of the wind below him.

"How far was that shot?"

"Hard to tell, a mile up there, not two," he said.

"Good." She looked up at him. "You're in with Yarnell."

"Hand me my pants. I'm not in with anybody." She threw the Levi's in his direction and he put them on.

"You lie." She shook her head. She held up his BlackBerry. "What's this?" Mack sat and cleaned his socks and carefully put them on and then his boots, tying them double. "You know he's a fucking crook."

"I don't know. I know he's slippery."

"Slippery? He is more of a mercenary than anyone we've ever known. Kent knows all about him and his little loaner air force."

"He should; they were partners."

"A long time ago. God, Mack! What the fuck are we doing up here? I'm making you a nap and you're on a fucking treasure hunt. Did you even want me to come?"

"Vonnie."

"Fuck you, mister man. Fuck you twice." She hauled back and threw the BlackBerry out and it fell into the lake ten feet from shore.

"Vonnie."

She turned to him. "No, fuck you. Why am I even saying? Good luck, you fucking patriot." He saw she had charged her vest with some of the food, granola bars, an apple. "I'm gone, Mack. If you see me in the post office, don't even say hello."

"Vonnie, don't do this."

"My phone's dead. Those guys were half a mile from Clark, right?"

"Right, straight west of Clark in the timber."

"I'll call from Crowheart. Don't follow me. I'm hiking out. Use the bag; I don't want it now. I only waited the hour to see you lie again." Vonnie picked up her fly rod. She started to drop down the rocks but caught herself, her sore leg, and turned to pass him and cut to the trail.

"How's your leg?" he said. She walked into the trees and was gone.

He stood in his boots. He knew what he had to do. He crossed quickly to the campsite and gathered what gear there was, caching the cookware between two large rocks and hanging his old coffee-pot in a branch in the third tree back. He rolled her sleeping bag and tied it tight and lodged it well up in the fourth tree. He looked down at his tent, but no way. Now he descended to the shore of Valentine Lake and skirted to where he saw the BlackBerry in the pellucid depths. He cut the leader off his fishing line and tied on a swivel and clipped on the biggest treble hook he had, along with a lead drop sinker. He tried it five times bumping the thing. When he reeled in the last time, it was to measure the depth. Sixteen feet. He stripped and folded his clothing high and dry on a rock the size of a desk by the water. The BlackBerry looked like it was four feet away in the shimmering curtain of sunlight. He took a breath and dropped into the water which was so cold he felt he was being crushed. Mack was never a good swimmer. He pushed down, feet first, and his ears hurt and still he went down, striking the thing with the sole of his foot and squeezing it there with the other until he could reach quickly, his ears snapping again, and grab it in his hand. He blew out and ascended and sputtered onto the rocks. His skin burned in the raw air and his head was full of water. He shook the BlackBerry and set it in the sun while he danced foot to foot. He knew it was waterproof, but he didn't know about sixteen feet in a lake at eleven thousand.

"Cold again," he said. "Wet again." He waved his arms and tried to dry his legs with his hands, gasping, and finally he just stood, back to the sun, his arms on the rock as if he were about to give a sermon naked to the massive sandstone scree while the chills ran up and down his skin. I am not an admirable man. What am I doing with a treble hook anyway? And that's just the start of it:

He dressed still wet and went above and the BlackBerry opened for him and read now: W. 39 degrees. The time was half an hour before. The blue dot was still flashing. The thing could receive underwater. He measured it out, put his hand up west thirty-nine degrees. He could get over there and look in two hours, turn and with no pack he could hike hard, fast and light, and reach the cars at the trailhead by nine P.M. It was the ranch; he had this one chance. If he hurried, he could still catch her. Or he could cut now and catch her before the valley rim and tell Yarnell he had looked. "Here you go," he said, and he turned west and started fast toward the big mountain.

All the way he stayed in the trees when possible and he watched for smoke. He wanted to see those kids' fire, but the sky was clear. It warmed to about fifty and he was sweating as he came to the first shoulder of Gannett Peak. He'd never climbed it, but he knew the maps: two shoulders then a rock saddle on the south side. He hated descending the first hill to get to the second, but the highline did not go where he was going. He was right on with the time.

At two hours he was startled by a shadow and stepped back to see an owl drift overhead motionless, a four-foot wingspan, looking for rock rabbits at the edge of the talus, onto which Mack now clambered. He stood and scanned the rocks, a trillion tons. If anything dropped here, it broke. Needle in a goddamn haystack. He had half an hour before he absolutely had to turn and go. He drank the rest of his canteen. He saw that he needed to go another quarter mile west so he could look back with the sun behind him. There was mica throughout and the field glinted at him in rolling rays as he walked. He had to watch his feet the whole way, but it was easy going and fast. When he reached the high point of the shoulder, he saw what he already knew: this wasn't the high point; it was still another horizon away. He struck for that and there was another. The curve of the planet. It was one bright world here, gray and silver and white and there were no cairns; he was well away from any traveled path. The air on his neck was cold and the sun on his face hot. If he stopped, he chilled and he sweated as he walked up the rocky platform.

He was as far from roads as you could get in this country and he had the old rare feeling of being the first person walking here and, a few minutes later, first person here. From the beginning of time. This tipped stone plateau was stark and indifferent; sometimes places revealed their indifference. They had been here eons and would be here eons. The rocks didn't care what happened to the man and they hadn't cared a thousand years ago and they wouldn't care in a thousand thousand. Everywhere around him now he saw rocks that didn't care and wouldn't care. It was exhilarating and Mack knew it was melodramatic. The sunlight here was ageless and indifferent too. Mack smiled.

He had to hurry. Vonnie was picking her way along the trail down. He felt certain she would stop and see Clay; they always checked out on the way. He could still scramble and catch her. And then? He couldn't make anything happen. He'd either shown her or not by now. Hope refused to die but it got real thin sometimes.

He was thinking of what he would say to Yarnell. *I walked the shoulder and in good light there was nothing east to west. I went over three quarters of a mile until I could see the western valleys. Nobody's going to find your trigger. It's lost. Can I see the*

*money? I ran across the last slope under the winter sun and it
was nevermore.*

"That thing is lost," he said aloud. Mack picked up his loping
strides and jogged along in the open day. Three, four, five minutes
slowing on the broken plates and standing again, now hands on
his knees, breathing heavily, while the blood snapped in his forehead. Looking out behind him, he could see the thickly treed
slopes over one valley and below at Upper Divide. He'd been there
last night or was it early this morning? Line of sight, he thought.
That's where his BlackBerry had started the signal. The water
registered in his ears and he tapped his head each way to try to get
any of it out. It was painful and then the device in his pocket vi-
brated and he started as if he'd been shocked and with it in his
hand, he saw the flashing blue dot.

It was here.

He stood still and scanned the rock mountain. It appeared a
wrinkled blank page. Then he saw something in the brilliant massive slope. He stood and folded his arms and squinted up, his heart
still hammering. Here, looking east so the shine was dulled, he
saw a splash of soot three hundred yards up, as if someone had
struck a giant match. He checked again and it was still strange, so
he started hiking, slowly this time, each step a knee burn. Well
below the black marks, there were glassine shards and small curls
of wire. The thing had blown. He gathered a handful of the stuff
and put it in a baggie. The black smears were hardened like tar and
at the upper side he found the impact point and there in the rock
crevasse were shorn spearpoints of chrome. He lay on the rocks
and could hear the mountain gurgling where the underground

water ran. It was constant there. He pulled the steel petals up and put them on the rock beside him. The place confused him, the huge black mar, and only this debris? He stood again on the strange angled table of rock.

There were so many times way out in the wild when Mack's eyes made human features or intricate and intentional designs out of a tangled wall of deadfall trees or urban scenes or houses from a slate slope of granite talus, and now he scanned the edge of the plateau at the twenty dwarf piñons growing in a knot sheltered by a rocky overhang and guarding their cache of snow, and he saw the silver plate of a tail fin. It was cut perfectly in the yellow day, but it didn't resolve into rock but grew into the girdered fuselage of the accident, so strange and dire that Mack took a step backward and put his hands on his knees, focusing for five seconds on his hiking boots and then back up at the bizarre picture.

Mack stepped rapidly up to the site and put his hand on the aluminum tail fin, and with the touch all of his confusion vanished. For some reason when he felt it in his hand, he called, "Hello!" And he knew immediately this was worse than he'd thought. There had been no fire. The silver craft was tucked into the slot of rocks and trees and cornice of the season's first snow as if parked there. It was much bigger than Mack had supposed, and he saw two things at once: the single triangular wing was made of light-gauge material and was some kind of liquid crystal display. He pressed his finger, and the material bled out, paled. They were screens of some kind; this was the invisible ultralight. The fuselage was a skeleton of girders. Mack pulled himself along the side, knowing what he would find in the tiny cockpit. The plane had somehow stalled and pancaked onto the mountain and the bottom was smashed. There was no canopy and the pilot, still wearing the oxygen mask, was crushed and bent over, so that Mack could easily press his knuckles into the neck where there was no pulse, just cold flesh. It was Chester Hance; Mack didn't even have to look twice.

Mack sat in the stones and leaned against the plane, breathing. No. He put his head in his hands and said, "Oh no." This was Yarnell's secret. He'd killed somebody with an airplane and now he wanted the airplane. Mack would help them find his friend and then he would tell everyone. He felt the moment now settle into his stomach like a stack of bricks. He fished the BlackBerry GPS out of his pocket and checked to see it was on. He slid it into the cockpit and saw that the console was broken into two pieces the size of decks of cards and he took those and stuffed them into his pack. Evidence. He put his hand on the pilot's shoulder and then took it back.

His father had taught him not to make two troubles into three by hurrying, but Mack stood and now he moved briskly down the pressed rock runway, careful of his footing, and then he said, "Don't run," and then he was running, telling himself it was okay, this was downhill and open and smooth. It hurt his thighs to govern his speed and he couldn't tell if he was running or simply trying to stop. Long strides. His ears were roaring and through that racket he heard a sound larger than his own eardrums and the underground stream, a gurgling that grew louder as if something were rolling down the hill toward him, a hollow ball knocking louder and then louder. He stopped himself with both arms against the first tree in the grove that bordered the granite highland, and he stood stock still, unable to place the sound as it became a loud vibrato and then the distinct clatter of a helicopter.

Mack stepped back into the shade and witnessed a glass ball rise over the rock horizon in the white sunlight, and he knew immediately it was the helicopter from Yarnell's field. A little glass two-man. It came up low over the western ridge and turned to the upper slope without mistake. For a minute he was glad to see it, and he thought his troubles were over. He could get down to Clay's in fifteen minutes. A two-man helicopter unmarked, low, faster now, right in the sun. He wished again for Vonnie's binoculars, but even so he could see Yarnell in the copilot's seat, no question because he was wearing his beautiful pink-checked shirt again. That was the trouble with those gold coast shirts; they were easy to remember. Mack could see Yarnell had a rifle across his lap. The little craft made a generous loop assessing the rock slope and then settled over the soot mark, as if they'd been there before. The wonders of GPS. Mack's head cleared: they'd received the signal hours before and raced over here and missed him by a minute. Mack had now backed farther into the copse. He hoped they couldn't land up there and would have to find a level and then hike up, because he needed time to escape, but he saw the helicopter set one strut on the ground and hold there, and after a moment Yarnell dropped a leg out and was going to descend.

Mack stood and dodged down through the growth, under the deadfall and onward, stopping against the first big tree with a full canopy. He wanted to make sure he wasn't hiding like a horse—as his father called it. Standing with their heads in the brush, the horses think they're hidden. And oddly, because they didn't move, they were hard to see, especially at twilight. He tried to still his breath and listen as the helicopter hovered. Yarnell would find the BlackBerry and know he was too late.

And then they would come looking for him.

Mack would have to wait. He couldn't cross open ground until they left. He looked at his watch: twelve-thirty. *You knew he was going to do this*, Mack thought, *and still you left the BlackBerry*. He pulled out his treasure, all the blasted bits of Yarnell's pieces, and put them into two baggies and zipped them into his pack's side pocket.

The machine's motors were steady for five or six minutes and then Mack heard it whine and the harmonics changed. He looked up through the branches as it grew fainter and fainter and he wished it to recede to nothing, but then he filled with terror as he heard it returning. It flew right over him and he needed to run now, but he made himself sit. The helicopter again orbited above his thicket and Mack sat still. He was surely out of sight in the deep trunk well of the old pine. It was so close and so loud. Yarnell was trying to scare him out. *They cannot see you*, he whispered. He was snugged against the trunk in the small space, and he put his pack on his lap and went through it. He had a light poncho and inside the cover he found a pouch of chocolate-covered coffee beans a year old and perfect. He ate them one at a time as the helicopter worked up and down the mountain valley. Twice the sound dissolved and then emerged. Then the noise was gone. He stood up and listened: nothing. The air moving across the sun-warmed sheet of rock made a white hum that also was indifferent to his life. Vonnie. She would have stayed on the trail. He'd dead-head cross-country and without a disaster, he could get to Clay in the elk hunters' tent a half hour ahead of her. *Here you go.*

Mack picked his way off the trail through the thick deadfall timber until he came to the lower edge of the field of trees. He wanted to run now, run and catch Vonnie and tell her the whole story, and he was clambering over the last big deadfall log about to step into the daylight when he heard something, a voice, Yarnell hollering. The light aircraft was standing stopped on the level rockface of the mountain saddle a hundred and fifty yards away.

"We know where you are, Mack."

You don't know where I am. You think I'm already on my way down. Mack rolled to look at his watch, and he knew that waiting like this was not what Yarnell could do, and he was right.

"Mack," the older man called again. "We're not done."

Mack knew that was true. He wondered there lying still, why not just walk out and give it up. Yarnell was not going to shoot him. Walk up and talk it over. Ride down to the trailhead in the thing. Then he remembered his father's way of turning face-on to men like Yarnell when he dealt with them at the ranch. How he sometimes had to move around to get them face to face. It was such a signal for Mack of his father's anger, and something ticked in Mack and he thought, *Don't you move.*

"Listen. You don't understand," Yarnell shouted. "You don't make it down."

Wait, just wait. In four minutes he heard the helicopter squeal to a start and rotor up over the four-acre strip of trees belting the mountain pass. He lay under the suspended log under the ferns and the canopy, and he thought Yarnell would rove and shoot perhaps, but he didn't shoot and the helicopter made three passes all very low and none of them near him on the downhill side and then it rose, laboring in the altitude and went west out of the mountains.

Mack stood and then sat on the ground feeling the heartbeat in his forehead. He moved on adrenaline over the open rock passage and entered the real forest again.

How he loved this range, these woods. He stopped every ten minutes and listened over his whistling breath, but there was no more helicopter. He was talking to himself, waving his arms. "Helicopter. How much bullshit is that? It's not in the book," he said. "The glass helicopter is not in the book. You're not in the book."

He didn't let his mind go back to Chester. He had to get down.

He stayed off the trail, climbing parallel to it and then he descended carefully counting switchbacks and there were twelve until he was in the long shadows of the upper meadow and he crossed the wooden bridge on the Wind and almost ran to the campsite on Valentine Lake. From there he surveyed the high wilderness valley: no smoke. He untied the clothesline and coiled the fifty feet of nylon cord into his pack. The sleeping bag and coffeepot were still in the trees. "I'll see you again," he said. In the lake he saw two fat forms pass over his old tent, rainbow trout in the late day. Then he left the main trail going the other way around Valentine, the hard way. It was up and over the rocks, but it was shorter if he could gut it out. He climbed the southern shoulder of the bald mountain, a thirty-degree staircase, stepping in his shadow every step, his shirt sweated to his back under the pack. He rounded the mountain and crossed the summit valley easily, weaving in and out of the aspen there on the high ground, his shadow tall and then taller. He looked up and said, "Don't get dark. Just wait." There were elk gathered in two of the meadows, thirty in one herd, stone still, their heads following him. When he topped the ridge and saw the eastern slope, the sun was gone. Here there was a good game trail all along the escarpment above Jamboree, a stream they said that flowed all the way to Lander. At points the worn path was a foot from the lip of the cliff, two hundred feet above the winding stream which he could not hear. Several times watching his footing, he walked right into trees where the elk had passed under and he had to go around. It was darker, but the hundred-mile horizon glowed. Vonnie was somewhere below him. She had water and candy and was walking carefully with her injured leg down the open trail in the last light. She'd regroup at the trailhead and straighten her car perhaps, waiting to see him.

Mack moved quickly along the path. This route led him two miles through some shallow hillocks to Lost Lake, where they had fished the second or third year. He had gone out to gather firewood and found an ancient wooden canoe banked against the hillside, two paddles and a lead rope lodged inside. They sat it in the lake a day to swell and that night paddled through the mirrored waters, catching fish. "We're the only people who have trolled in the upper lakes of the Winds," he had told her.

"Except for the guy who hauled it up here."

"It's Hiram's," Mack said. "He only uses it for exercise."

Now Lost Lake was still in the new night. He knew where there were three good Mepps spinners in a hollow log across at the old campground. He was full of ghosts.

He followed the outlet down to Prairie Lake where one year

they'd come across a woman curled in a campground while her husband fished. Vonnie talked to her and found that her period had started and she was miserable. They'd given her Vonnie's cure: an ounce of Jack Daniel's and a NoDoz. In those days Vonnie always brought a half pint of the whiskey which they had in their coffee at night. Prairie was a silver plate now and the night had become cold. He struck from the end of the lake cross-country up and over the two ridges where, later than he thought, he joined the main trail. He loved the moment of crossing onto a recognized trail. When he hit it, he wanted to run, but he held himself. You think you can see, but you cannot. It's dark, buddy. No running in the dark. "No running period," he said aloud. He walked fast. He was a mile above the big meadow. The dark meadow was trouble. Not the stream which he stepped right through, but with no moon it was hard to keep the trail and he fell twice and then slowed down, high-stepping the sage.

He approached Clay's tent close and called, "Hello the camp!"

"Yo" came the return and Clay appeared. "Mack, you're late. I just ate, but come on, I'll open another can." Mack crossed and entered the warm shelter. The tent smelled like Dinty Moore stew and the two men looked at each other. Mack felt his eyes adjust in the hissing lantern light.

"Where's Vonnie?" Mack said.

"Okay, Mack," Clay looked at him. "Where is she?"

Clay tried to talk Mack into sitting still, waiting, spending the night. "She'll be along," he said. "She's got a flashlight and knows this trail. Give it an hour. She'll be here."

"She might, but I'm going back up."

"Where's your pack?" He told Clay about the poachers and their location so he could radio in the report.

"She wouldn't have run into them," Clay stated, "if they were by Upper Divide."

"I need fresh socks and a shirt," Mack said. "Do you have any salt tablets?"

"Gatorade in the cooler." Mack sat at the little picnic table in the elk hunters' tent and changed clothes and drank a cup of cold coffee and a quart of blue Gatorade and refilled the bottle with water. Clay gave him a nylon bivy sack.

"I won't need this," Mack said.

"I know," Clay said, "that's why you're taking it."

Mack stuffed the little cloth tube into his pack. He thought about telling Clay about the helicopter but no.

"I'm just going up there a quarter mile to Cold Creek where she'll be standing perplexed about how to cross without getting her feet wet and we'll come down and eat the rest of your stew."

"Sounds like a plan. You want a gun?" Clay pointed to the two holstered pistols hanging from the pan rack.

"No, I'd hurt myself. But my light is dead."

Clay retrieved his strapped headlamp and showed him how to turn it on. "Brand-new batteries," he said.

"Perfect. I'm golden." Mack stood and shouldered his daypack and adjusted the lamp on his forehead. "See you in a minute."

"I'll be here," Clay said. "Be careful."

The temperature in the great night had fallen another ten degrees, and when Mack looked up, his headlight beam was swallowed by the void. There was nothing between him and the four trillion stars except the unending waves of dark chill dropping steadily onto the mountain meadow. The headlight lit the trail perfectly in a three-foot oval and he stepped carefully up the path and across the stepping-stones in Cold Creek. He went up the hill into the forest again and he wanted to see Vonnie coming down or find her sitting on a log taking a break. Every stride matches hers coming down, he thought. We'll meet very soon. He thought about whether she might already be below, starting her car, wheeling around for the drive down. He didn't think so, but if she were, he was making a long walk in the dark for nothing. No, she would have stopped and seen Clay.

It took him two hours to reach the summit rim and descend into the high mountain valley. Badgers were working darkness all along the way; they'd look at the light and waddle into the rocks. He turned his light off in the willow meadow and could almost see the trail; it was open there, but when he entered the forest, he had to turn it on. "Hi Vonnie," he said aloud, walking and talking. "Just where have you been? Well, hello Vonnie. It's dark and Clay's got the soup on. Vonnie, that I was impossible to live with does not alter the fact that I love you and would like to try again. No, I mean, Vonnie, I'm happy you've found a responsible and resourceful partner and I hope he is kind to you for the rest of your days. Me, I'm just a broken townie. No, I know I burned my bridges, but didn't you know I'd swim back across."

Then he was up and over the little hill that led down to the Wind River. He could hear it in the night. He didn't want to run into the moose now, but he never got the chance. Suddenly there were a lot of tracks on the trail, a parade of big feet. He back-tracked them to the little trail's turning. He hadn't seen this tiny trail the day they'd gone in.

And then he saw her rod, at least the tip of it. There on the trail was the broken foot-long end piece of her precious bamboo fly rod. She had broken it off right here and stepped on it. He squatted and turned off his lamp. Hi Vonnie. Where are you? Who are you with? In his concentration, he imagined the picture of her held or struggling with Canby and his sidekick. He wanted now to run, to yell, and so he sat still. He took off the headlamp and held it in his hand as he followed the little trail out along the mountainside toward the poachers' camp. He didn't want it on his head anymore. This way, when they shot, it wouldn't be between his eyes. There was no hurry now and he tried not to hurry. The trail was printed heavily with boots and hardened in the few hours since they'd been created. He followed it up to the landslide and stopped, breathing quietly, and then he decided to climb over for the prospect. If they had a fire, he could see it from on top. He turned off the lamp and started, but as soon as he crawled onto the rocks, he dislodged one, and it rolled and then another moved, and there was no way to get over this without a big fanfare. They'd think a car was coming. He slid down and stood. Was he panicked? He checked his watch. Five minutes after midnight. He sat down and turned on the lamp and checked his hands. Muddy but okay. He wasn't nicked up. He wasn't panicked. His heart now was in his jawbone, but he wasn't panicked. Too much. Okay, then. He reassumed the path and walked down around the rock spill and the crazy trees, light off, carefully. On the other side he could see nothing. It was dark in the woods, and where he could see through to the mountain, it was darker. Two hundred yards, and he got on his hands and knees and felt the boot prints still. He was close. He could hear nothing except the omnipresent air as the earth turned and the throbbing felt concussion of his heart. He was goddamned close. He was too close and he sat down and thought, tried to think.

Then he crawled forward on his hands and knees. He knew he was in trouble because he couldn't tell how much time had passed. This was no good. He made a step and then another. The trail had widened and he made another step. He put his hand on a tree and stepped to the next, put his hand there. Tree by tree, he moved until he put his hand on the head of a tenpenny nail. He froze and opened his eyes as wide as they would work, trying to make out forms on the ground, the old tent, anything. Again he was aware he didn't know how long he had been there. He was standing in the butchers' camp; he knew it without any further evidence. He could smell blood. Somehow suddenly he lifted the headlamp and turned it on. And off. The three shapes had stunned him and he lighted the space again. The three gutted elk hung from the bar, but the camp was empty. A dozen cans littered the cold fire ring and there were strips of red cord around the area and bright wood chips and dirty rags. He studied the perimeter, the old log that had been a bench, behind which were cigarette butts and Vienna sausage tins, the ten trees, every one with a nail or two. The ribs of the elk in their open chests were bright in the light. She would have left something here, somehow. He turned off the lamp and stood in the center of the abandoned camp. They came in here this afternoon. She sat there. Where. Not on the log. In front of it. Who else is here? She had her daypack. Would they tie her hands?

She'd sit on the ground. He got on his hands and knees in front of the bare log and shined the lamp underneath. The shiny thing pressed into a seam in the wood was her ring. Mack put his forehead against the smooth old deadfall and closed his eyes. Her beautiful ring. He put it in his pocket.

He quit the camp and crossed the trail, dropping down the hillside a hundred yards where it became a steep declivity under a thick stand of pines that had dropped their billions of needles for three hundred years. There were pockets of mulch here two feet deep. Mack found a shelf and kicked a duff bed. There'd be no fire. He was no longer cold, but it would be serious tonight, freezing. He pulled his boots off and slipped into the bivy sack on the soft deck of needles. He pulled cakes of the stuffing in fistfuls up over his bed. He sat up and drank some water. When he lay down his ears sizzled with the lake water again. A day. Vonnie was wearing shorts, but she had her fleece and her vest. She was strong. She would be strong.

Day Six

An eight-point buck was stepping through the deep dawn, each step a muted crash in the thick tinder. He passed twenty feet from Mack, who watched him unmoving. The light was the same as it had been at the bottom of the lake, magnified and undisturbed, a grotto. The deer was in no hurry and disappeared seamlessly into the fifty shades of gray at this hour. Mack sat up and listened. Frost lay in paisley patterns throughout the wood, wherever it could set unimpeded by the branch cover. He couldn't hear a thing and his ears burned sharply now with the lake water. He couldn't tap it out but tried. "I'm right here," he said to the world, and he drank from his canteen and started for the trail. It was five-ten A.M. and maybe twenty-five degrees. He had no plan.

The elk hung unmoving in the abandoned camp and he went through, glad to be leaving no tracks in the frozen dirt. He walked the narrow trail along the treeline, a gentle up and down ringing the mountain. A mile later it dropped and crossed a game park clogged with tall willows. At the bottom it crossed the Dubois trailhead path and there was a new Forest Service sign with an arrow that said eight miles. His own trail departed that and narrowed and almost disappeared except for yesterday's boot tracks in the leaves. Frost was general. Mack scanned the sky and there were no markings. The sun had not yet clipped the far peaks. Now the path was only a deer trail and the thick cover offered no forward view, bush to bush. Mack pushed through as it led across the valley and into a canyon he hadn't perceived. He stood and took it in, another mystery in his mountains. Even at the narrow mouth the cliff sides were steep, some fissure in the ancient topography, a shift when the continent settled. The corridor was about as wide as a two-lane road and choked with scrubby piñon and aspen protected from the open world. A rill he could step over ran down the center of this place and he could see, as he ascended, where the party had crossed and recrossed the pretty waterway. He liked lost places like this, private surprises not seen by a dozen pioneers; there were thousands of secluded recesses in the wild and they filled him with hope, always. Until now. The canyon narrows and the tiered rocky walls grew taller, the slice of pale blue morning sky closing to a slash above him.

They'd encountered plenty of campers on their trips, a group or two every year. Two political science professors from UCLA last year, on sabbatical they said, camped at Vernon Lake. They'd all had coffee of an afternoon, and the guys went on and on about their recipes for trout. They had bags of piñon nuts and almonds and the like along with beautiful heavy cookware, the kind you don't see unless it's a horse trip. The one guy showed off his little handheld battery-operated device that slivered almonds. Vonnie kept trying to talk flies and they didn't care about the fishing, just steaming the fish and olive oil. She told them truly about hanging all their comestibles in a bear bag, and the men looked annoyed. They didn't want to put everything away every night; this was a two-week trip. But it was astonishing coffee, and they were better outdoorsmen than most. When they left, Vonnie said, "When the bear walks into that camp, he's going to think he died and went to heaven."

Vonnie and Mack also came across the various outfitters they knew, Richard Medina from Cody, who'd take on a late trip for a bonus, some family from Paris who wanted to ride horses in and see the big mountains, *grande région sauvage de montagne!* Mack knew all ten of Medina's horses by name from half a mile, and they greeted Medina himself *sauvage de montagne* happily every time their paths crossed. They also ran into the Eds, Ed Carey and Ed Wooten, from Jackson, who always laughed about seeing them because they'd given them two cans of beer the first time. Outfitters always had a beer horse, and the Eds accused Vonnie of following them to get her allotment of Budweiser. "One taste and she's a groupie," they'd laughed.

One year, the third or fourth September, they met three kids coming down in the open scree and one had broken his radius in a fall. They'd been weekending from school in Salt Lake, a three-day weekend and the boy had slipped at the summit. The boy was walking shock, and Vonnie sat him down. The other boys were jolly and giving their friend a bit of a ride. They wanted to get to the truck and go to Starbucks. The kid himself was gray and cold. Mack could see the bone under the skin, but it hadn't broken through. When he had said give me your phone, they'd all three fished out cells, even the wounded boy. They called the Crowheart store and arranged for EMTs to be at the trailhead.

"It will take them two hours to get there and be waiting," Vonnie said, "which is perfect for you. It's two miles to your car, and then a ten-mile drive down the dirt road to the highway. Keep this guy between you." She turned to the injured boy. "How do you feel?"

"Sick," he said.

"Let's have some water and take a rest." She pointed at Mack and said, "My partner has a cure-all we should drink." Mack had walked down and filled his liter bottle from the stream and shook up the powdered lime drink.

"It's good for broken arms," the boy said.

"Any bone," Mack had said, "especially the skull. But your head looks okay." The boy drank from the bottle greedily and again and then he lay back and they covered his legs.

"Is it bad?" his friend said.

"Everyone is going to be okay, but you're going to lose your fishing net to the cause." She cut out the netting and made an arm sling. In half an hour the kid had finished the bug juice and had a little pink in his cheeks. She told him, "All you have to do is walk this trail for an hour. There's no climbing." She looked up at the two other boys. "And take your time. When you get to the meadow, sit down again for ten minutes before you get in the car. It's hard not to hurry, but don't hurry."

"You want us to go with them?" Mack asked her.

"He's okay," she said. "You play baseball?" she asked the boy.

"No."

"Too bad," she told him. "You're going to have an amazing right arm in ten weeks."

And one year they had pulled into the trailhead and surprised a couple making love in the afternoon. The two had scrambled up for their clothes, and after a funny long-distance discussion across the space, they came over and ended up having some of the pasta with Mack and Vonnie as the night fell.

But they'd never met madmen. Some folks had handguns and said so, for bears they were always quick to say, and the outfitters had their scabbard rifles, but just for show.

Mack stopped and saw that he had lost the trail. He went side to side in the narrows and it was right there but untracked. "Shit," he said. "Just shit." He scanned 360 degrees, the light was new ribbons everywhere in the gray and the green, a puzzle. He started back down. At fifty yards he came to the hidden turning. The branches were broken, and the leaves tracked clearly. Hard to miss; he was quite the woodsman. There was a fork here, a broken alley in the cliffside that was apparent from above. Go slow, he said. He walked through the golden aspen grove around the corner into the gloomy side canyon. Here the shade was actually purple, and the aspens twisted upward through three seasons: green leaves at the bottom, yellow in the middle, and their top branches already bare. It was step by step now and slow, until at the second corner, and the new room opened wider and Mack saw an optical illusion or thought he did. The tangled gray deadfall timber that was everywhere resolved itself into a shed, a shack. He stepped back and crouched, wishing he had Vonnie's field glasses now.

It was a log hovel, one small marred glass window in front. The gray plank door, he determined, opened inward. No smoke from the crude rock chimney. Who knew? he thought. This had been here seventy years at least, built by some ardent misanthrope. As he sat, he heard something coming from the place, from behind it, like digging and he heard the unmistakable lip blow of a horse. Horses. Keeping his eye on the door, he edged around the far side of the shelter against the canyon wall, forty feet away. He stayed low and the melted frost on the brush soaked him. The old logs had settled hard in the structure and there were no windows except that in the door. There were three horses, and he was surprised that they were good horses, groomed and well fed. They appeared to be horses he might know, but they weren't. He didn't approach. All the tack was slung over two huge bare logs. The animals regarded him calmly, and he noted the raw horse trail leading up the draw behind. They must have come in from below Dubois. Behind them in a tree hung another gutted elk. There was a haystack of antlers to one side, hundreds. These guys were going after it. He was out of sight south of the coarse homestead and it was almost eight o'clock, but he knew absolutely not what to do. He crouched and then sat and waited. His legs went to sleep and then he shifted and waited.

Chester Hance had learned to be a pilot, and he had been a careful guy, not a roughneck, and he had flown Yarnell's new planes. That wing had been a screen of some kind. The body had been there over a week. Mack closed his eyes and folded himself tight. Yarnell had left him there over a week.

At the hour of nine the door screamed and opened and the heavyset man came out wearing brown field coveralls with the straps folded down. He went back in and came out struggling into his canvas jacket. He had a bucket and walked out of sight toward the main canyon. Mack was hidden but he thought about it now, being between the two men, trapped. He should get up and get out and call the police. He was trapped in a stupid place. A minute later the man came back spilling the bucket as he walked. He went in and Mack heard the door crash shut. It probably still had the leather hinges.

He needed a SWAT team; this was stupid. A day out and a day back, even with horses. He thought it all over, and then he made his decision. He would wait. He considered calling to the camp, just walking up and trying to talk it all off. No, it was past talking. Trouble was another language and he'd glimpsed it on the dark road of last year with the drugs and no measure of reason or grace. He'd been hit in the head twice by people who didn't even bother to swear. There had been no reason either time except that he was in arm's reach. The crudeness was breathtaking. One had been a woman and he still had the mark beneath his cheekbone where her ring had struck. These people didn't talk. No, now he would wait. He'd never been good at it, but now it was his only choice. If there was a scream, he'd go in.

An hour later the same man came out and went around to the horses. He was working there a long time and then he led the red horse, now saddled, to the side and tied the reins to a sapling. Then he disappeared for another forty minutes and saddled the brown horse and brought it over. This horse work was new to him, evidently. "Wes," he called to the cabin. "Wes!" The door squealed again and the younger man, Wes Canby, came out dressed right out of the Gap in a green jacket and clean khakis. He wore new two-tone hiking boots, almost dress boots. He'd shaved, though not well. These guys had drugs in their faces if you knew where to look. The hollow line beneath the cheekbone, a withered draw that sometimes showed the contours of the teeth; their narrow faces were suffering. Wes Canby was carrying two rifles and he stood on the edge of the step and waited for his partner to negotiate mounting the brown horse. When he was up, the young man handed him the guns and checked the cinch, setting it a notch tighter. He adjusted the other saddle. Mack was watching the open doorway. He wanted now to call, but it was no good. He could do a goose, that was his best, but there were no geese up here. They were too smart to fly this high. He could do a horse, but not from here. Besides, everybody in Jackson had a whinny on their cellphones now and the horse was about ruined. He could do a pika; she'd know that, the chirp. He readied and then chickened out. He didn't know if she was even in there.

The young man said something to the other man, and he walked over and pulled the door to, again with a clap, and now he ran a piece of thick outfitters rope through the iron handle and out around the old aspen in front of the door and he doubled it and tied a hitch, snugging it plenty. He mounted the red horse and led the two of them around the cabin and up the draw.

You wait, Mack whispered to himself. You just wait. He looked at his watch and said: twenty minutes more. Just sit. He could feel the tops of his legs aching from all that downhill when he was running from the helicopter. Would Yarnell have shot me? He shook his head. When he stood, he heard the clear concussions of a horse stepping down the trail, and he crouched again and listened to the approach, the red horse suddenly coming around the front of the wooden house. The young man's hair was blown back and he was smiling. He stepped the horse around the front of the place back and forth and he leaned and checked the rope, and then he turned and heeled the horse again up the trail. Mack stood and went to the corner of the shack and watched the man disappear, and then he followed, walking up the trail carefully but with some speed, three hundred yards to where it switched back for the ridge. The men were gone.

Back at the cabin, he went to the door and said, "Vonnie."

"Mack," she said. He heard her say it again. "Be careful." He untied the knots and looped the rope through. He had to kick the door to get it to open into the small dark space. "Here," she said, and he went to her on the floor in a twisted blanket pile, horse blankets he could smell, and then the other girl cried out.

"It's okay," Vonnie said. "He's ours." They were both tied knees and elbows, pretty effectively for two poachers, he thought, but they would have mastered knots. Vonnie was crying now, softly.

"Did they hurt you?"

Vonnie shook her head, but her eyes were funny.

"Yes," the girl said.

"Where are your friends?"

"They ran down yesterday about noon," Vonnie told him. "They got away. This is Amy." The girl was crying, and she started at every sound.

"They hurt me," she said. "I want to wash. Oh god."

"We're going to go," Mack told her. "You're fine now. When are they coming back?" he asked Vonnie.

"They said they weren't; that we were going to die here."

"They're coming back," he said. "They left a horse."

"I need to wash," Amy said. "I can't go. God god god."

"Were they high?" Mack said.

"The big guy," Vonnie said. "He was nuts. Nuts." She was crying. That was the difference between them; she could cry and cope, but when he cried, he couldn't cope. He held her chin for a second and looked in her face: "Are you okay?"

"Yes, good." If she hadn't added the *good*, he would have believed the lie, but there would be no discussion now. "Where'd you go?"

"I'm sorry I let you go alone. Come on," he said.

"No," the young woman said. Amy would not let Mack help her. Amy would not get up from the floor until Vonnie helped her. Mack slipped out into punishing daylight and went around to the horse. He saw something and looked up where the men had ridden. Nothing. He was tired and run with fatigue, and his eyes were popping, but he hurried anyway. Would that guy come back and check twice? There was a bridle and a horse pack but no saddle.

"What's your name, fella?" he asked the horse. He walked the animal around to the front of the hovel. When the women emerged, the fact of two of them made him know how much trouble they had. There'd been a crime and another and it seemed he was in the middle of some way of avoiding another. He'd come upon stark accidents and tried to assemble the best pieces, but this was all migrating under his feet, and Mack worked to move slowly, and measure it all with care. He gave the women some water and he ran the rope back to the door and tied the knots again cinching them hard. He put Amy in front of Vonnie on the packhorse, and he led the black horse down to the pretty little rivulet and along the heartbreaking autumn canyon. They proceeded without talking along the mountain trail, good time, the horse steady and unperturbed. They'd left quite a trail, but he knew that time was on their side. This was the lightest load this horse had had in years. The day was clear and cold, but the sun helped and the walking was easy. When they came out of the trees and into the Wind River meadow, Mack said to Vonnie, "I got your ring."

At the summit he led the horse down and handed Vonnie the reins. "Give me your binocks," he said. She pulled the field glasses from her pack. "This horse's name is now Buddy. Take him on down and I'll catch you. Just stay on the trail. I want to have a look-see."

He was grateful to be over the crest, over the sight line. He watched the two women on the horse moving down the slope; from here they'd be easy to see for a long time. He crawled back into the rocks, keeping his head in the crenellated notches between boulders and scanned the vast noontime valley. This was the world he loved, and he checked with himself. *Something very bad has happened, boy. How do you feel about the place now?* In the magnified field of the powerful glasses the ridges jumped out, and he could see entire valleys he'd never fished. *I still love it.* They were terrific lenses and they gathered everything. He scanned down to where they'd come, tracing slowly the trail, and as he was glassing the far meadow, he saw the two men come out of the trees on their horses. They weren't running, but they were moving along. The young guy could ride, though part of it was carelessness, but the other guy was awkward and overworking the horse. He could see their faces vividly and the young guy was a picture of stark determination, studying the trail, and Mack could see the mask pressed over: drugs. The guy had a meth grin, stiff and pasty. They both had sidearms and there was a scabbard and a rifle butt protruding from the far side of Wes Canby's horse. It was the first time in his life that Mack knew that if he had a gun, he would simply wait hidden and shoot them both at close range.

Okay, he had to go.

Buddy was doing just fine through the rocks, following the struck path, and running again, Mack caught them and led the horse in a quick step down across the granite moonscape onto the forest switchbacks. He wanted to be in the trees. Amy was still crying in Vonnie's arms, leaning back, her red hair on Vonnie's shoulder. Through the forest the horse kept a pace up the hills and down, three hills and then the long one down into the meadow. The horse didn't stop to drink from Cold Creek but splashed through behind Mack and into the open meadow above Clay's tent. Halfway down Mack called to the lodge.

Clay came out and waved. "A horse," he said when they came up. "And two women." Amy had stopped crying now and Vonnie helped her off the horse.

"I brought you some trouble, Clay."

"Okay."

"Get these women something to eat, if you can. What working rifles have you got out here?"

"Just the Winchester. We'll have an arsenal tomorrow when the crew arrives."

"Have you got bullets?"

Clay pulled the rifle off the pegs where it hung on the tent's crossbeam and opened it. "It's a one-shot antique," he said. "But good as gold." He opened the ammo can and Mack picked out the bullets, ten of them. "It cocks like this and you're loaded," Clay showed him. Vonnie sat the girl at the table and put the teakettle on the stove. When she looked at the men and the open rifle, Mack took the gun and led Clay outside.

"Do you know what you're doing, Mack?" Clay asked him.

"Show me again." Mack asked his friend. Clay cocked the rifle open and chambered the shell, and then opened the breech again.

"Like so."

"Got it." Mack set the rifle against the tree and went into the tent. He sat by Vonnie at the big table and said, "You okay?" She couldn't hold his gaze, dropping her eyes. "They hurt you."

"They did. They both tried."

He took her hand. He couldn't feel anything; it was like when he'd been drugging. Everything was off, over there. He watched his hand let go of her. "Thanks for saying." He stood up. "I know what I need to know," he said to Clay.

Outside he hefted the rifle. "Good enough, and you've got your pistols."

"I do; just let me know."

"There's two guys," Mack said, "and I'm going to ride up and talk to them right now."

"Want me to come?"

"Just stay and keep an eye out. What did the sheriff say?"

"He said he's got a man going in from Dubois and to let him know what we see."

"Well, radio and tell him they're here. I shall return." He ducked inside the roomy tent another moment and kissed Vonnie on the cheek before coming out into the last daylight.

"Oh, Buddy," he said, swinging aboard the horse and grabbing the reins. "Let's go see those other horses." He hadn't barebacked since a boy and so he rode slowly up the meadow, the rifle across his lap. He felt like a boy, a feeling he'd had too often in the last two years, but his heart now was just a fire. He was doing something stupid again, but he would do it all the way. They'd hurt Vonnie and there was nothing for it. He rode the horse up through the open woodland in the weak sunlight. He could feel the fall, a season that he loved. God, it was a beautiful day in the world. He rode to the upper edge of the meadow and waited at the edge of the trees looking up into the pathway which was striped dramatically with tree shade in a laddered column. His heart was on, jolting him, and he could feel the concussion in his jaw as he tried to be still. He opened his mouth.

Above, the trail was a flickering print of light and shadow, a teeming display of what seemed people coming at every second, now and now. He could not ride into the trees, and he shook his head in sad wonder at this limit, this vigilance and fear. He thought he might ride in and hide and destroy these men, but now he was making his stand. Just wait, he said finally. They'll be along.

Finally the cascade of shadows stuttered and a form appeared at the top of the lane, a man and a horse, the larger man, two hands on the pommel, turning his chestnut horse down toward Mack, continuing. Mack watched behind the man, but no other figure appeared. Something was off about this.

"What is it," Mack said aloud to himself.

The man on the horse looked then and saw Mack below, eighty yards, and he arched in the saddle to get his hand on his sidearm. Mack watched him, and the man did not turn to see if his partner were coming, and then Mack knew the younger man, Canby, had gone the other way. Mack swiveled and looked back down the meadow, but the white tent was obscured by the trees, almost half a mile below. Now the man before him was twisting in his saddle to extract his pistol which was binding in the untethered holster. Mack couldn't move. *When he gets that gun out, he's going to cock it and walk his horse down here and shoot me.* The thought was just a thought, and Mack watched the horse come forward happily to see his old friend Buddy.

At twenty yards the man jerked his pistol free and almost

threw it with the effort, but he was new to guns and had to pull it
before his face with both hands the way a person studies a cell-
phone, and then evidently he mastered it and set it forward in the
air, aiming the revolver, a long-barreled Colt, Mack could now see,
at Mack. The gun was waving, but the man was getting closer and
it would be hard to miss very soon. Mack heard something on the
wind then, a cry, a sharp short cry, which sounded like Vonnie
screaming the word *no*, and it was enough to cause Mack to swing
his own rifle up in an arc and catch the barrel stock in his left palm
and then as he started moving it all became natural, his lifting the
gun up around toward the oncoming rider who was stepping with
his pistol through the splintered sunlight, and then Mack heard
two shots and then a third shot from below, two different guns,
and then he heard his own rifle explode as he pulled the trigger and the big man jumped back in his saddle, his head following
his bloody shoulder in a terrific fall to the ground. Mack had seen
men fall from horses, and he always hated it. It was never a stunt.
This was a big man to fall so far, wheeling off the horse's rump,
and he struck his head and shoulder on the rocky trail and lay
there unmoving.

Mack was surprised at how calm the horses were, stepping
sharply with the report and then standing to wait. They'd been
around guns. He pulled Buddy around and leaned on it and
nudged the black horse into a gallop through the sage, four, five
great leaping strides, and then he thought better of it and held the
horse back. He could go down two ways: through the meadow
openly or behind on the ridge trail, which was how Canby had
gone. He had to make a decision now and considered walking down the edge of the meadow out of sight which would take

longer but would ensure surprise. Then he heard one more shot and a scream and another scream, Vonnie this time, and another scream. He sat up and then bent again into the neck of the black horse and kicked him up into a gallop. There was care and then there was this. It didn't matter which way. He had to go. It didn't matter if he came off the horse, thrown; and because it no longer mattered, he knew he would not fall.

Before he came in sight of the tent, riding easily the black horse that ran fluidly and without fuss, Mack heard another shot, and he started to ease up, straightening from where he'd been against the horse's neck, the rifle clipped under his leg against the horse. Now he realized he had heard the bullet pass over his head, a whispering snap, a sound he'd never heard, and he noted it: That's how it is. It either hits you or misses you. He now could see the tent and out from it a ways the rider Canby reset his rifle for another shot. The man's beautiful red horse seemed confounded stepping in circles and Canby was focused on his efforts to square the rifle and shoot Mack who was riding still right into it. Mack had closed to thirty yards. Mack's mind went out. Everything jumped to two dimensions and lost order; was this wrong? Each second opened like the page of a crazy book. Behind the rider he could see the two women bent in the shadow of the tent, and Mack knew that Clay was down. Mack hauled Buddy up sharp with the reins and dropped a leg off the back of the horse and stood on the ground, swatting the horse away from the trail to be free from harm. Go go. As he landed, Mack felt his rifle bite into the dirt, the barrel; he felt it like doom. But it was good to be aground. Here he was. Now the page turned: the approaching horse in a half run at him; the horse was reluctant to run at a man, and there was something openly insane in these minutes, that phrase came through his head and he nearly said it. Canby's horse was odd, the reins dangled, and the man still had not righted his rifle. He was so close Mack could smell the horse. Canby kicked Mack in the chest as he went by and Mack went down hard in the dry sage and he could smell and feel it hard, and he woke and he knew he was stupid again.

Mack stood and knocked his rifle barrel against the side of his boot while he turned and looked up the meadow where Canby wheeled around on the red horse. *Your barrel is fouled, big boy. You're naked in the wind.* Mack knocked it again and then lifted and cocked the rifle and the shell flew out; it was already cocked. He wanted to take a minute to blow in the breech, but an explosion in the dirt at his feet stopped him and he fumbled a bullet from his pocket, lodged it in the chamber and closed the trigger guard. He stood in the trail and the horse saw him and came walking down.

"You dumb fuck," Canby said. He pointed at Mack and a smile creased his face. "It's time you gave me the trigger. All the shit you took from the plane." Without choice Mack took a knee. His vision rolled, and he felt his heart rinse. He stood up immediately and felt the blood pound his neck.

Mack heard the chamber of Canby's rifle snick charged. It would be a repeater of some kind. He hated rifles. "But," the young man said, "you stole a horse." He laughed and the laugh was all wrong, forced and hurting. "And you're a mile into the Wyoming wilderness. State land. Starts. A mile below." He raised an arm to point the way, and he almost fell off the horse. "You dumb fuck climbed around for Yarnell and then stole a horse in Wyoming—which is bad news. You're mine."

Mack felt the rock of his stomach, sick with fear, but he'd been sick a long time today about how all this kept growing, how he hadn't been in the right place, not even once, how he'd let it all happen.

The young rider, walking his horse toward Mack, brought his rifle up to his shoulder.

Mack had planned to say his name, issue some kind of threat, but his mind was white. The old rifle felt perfect now but as he swung it, he knew it might still be clogged and blow up in his face, but regardless he aimed for exactly one second and pulled the trigger. The shot was a flat crack as loud as anything a person gets to hear, and Canby went back off his horse as if he'd been hit with a shovel. Mack closed his eyes tight and when he opened them, the pages were gone, the rush of scattered light. His horse stood the ground, unmoving. These horses, Mack thought. Stand still in trouble.

Mack's horse walked out through the tall sage and joined the red bay, touching faces. Mack knelt and picked up the bullet he'd dropped and put it in his pocket. He knelt and laid the rifle across his knees and vomited. Twice. Breathing deeply and blowing hard, he strode up to where the man lay on his back in the fall flora. The bullet had hit his sternum dead center and ruined his body completely and he was dead. There was another bullet wound up under his right arm that had bled heavily through his shirt and into his pants. Mack didn't touch him. He mounted Buddy bareback rather than get in the other saddle and he led the red horse slowly down the meadow.

"Mack," he heard Vonnie call his name before he saw her. She and the girl were cutting the leg off Clay's pants. He was gray, his face a grimace, and he lay in the grass outside the tent. Clay pointed. "Just the leg," he said.

"Twice," Vonnie said.

"Did you radio?" Mack asked.

"Vonnie did."

Mack pulled the pantleg free and sliced it into two strips. He used his kerchief to wipe Clay's leg and noted that the wounded man did not recoil. The two wounds were welling, the one above the knee more than the other in the calf. They were angry red and dark and not really bleeding very much. Vonnie had taken the girl into the tent.

"I shot him," Clay said calmly.

Mack tied off the tourniquet mid-thigh, and the blood ebbed. "Move your foot up and down," Mack told his friend. He watched the foot rock back and forth. "Amazing. You still work." He examined the wounds again and saw that the bullets had not gone deep. "You're just plugged, Clay, but I'm not going to dig them out. Where were you?"

"In the tent. I saw him riding out back in the trees and went in and he shot through the goddamned tent. How crude is that."

"Miserable," Mack said. "But it sure slowed those slugs."

"Fucking tent shooter," Clay said.

"I shot him," Mack said.

"I shot," Clay said.

"You winged him, Clay. I shot him dead."

Clay studied Mack's face.

Vonnie came out of the tent with two blankets. She put the rolled one under Clay's head and opened the other over him. "I'll get some water," Mack said. He went into the canvas lodge and retrieved the med kit and returned and padded both wounds with compresses and surgical tape. He cut off the tourniquet.

When Vonnie had gone back inside, Mack held the canteen to Clay and said, "I shot both of them. I shot the big guy and he's laying right up there at the top of the park. I think he's just hurt. I shot the other guy dead. His name is Wes Canby, and he was holed up in Rawlings mostly; I knew him from my crimes driving drugs. He's dead."

Vonnie came out with both hands around a mug of milky coffee and handed it to Mack.

"Thank you kindly," he said.

"None for you," she said to Clay, "until after your airplane ride." Mack could see she had washed her face and combed her hair back. Vonnie looked at him and looked away. "You're pale." She waited and then smiled and said, "Now you say, 'You're pale.'"

"You're okay, Vonnie."

"You're okay, Mack."

"Trouble," he said. "But you're safe." It was two miles to the car in the last daylight, so he just said, "You guys go. You'll make the car by dark. I'll see you."

Amy came out of the tent tying her sweater around her waist. "Thank you," Amy said. She wouldn't look at them. "For coming to get us."

Mack only nodded.

"You want in the tent, Clay? Mack, should we help you move him in?"

"I'm good right here," Clay said. "Somebody has gone ahead and ruined my pants good, but the copter should be along in fifty minutes. Last year we had a compound leg and it was forty-one minutes from Jackson which was a record they wanted to put in the papers."

Vonnie knelt and kissed his cheek and she and the girl turned and walked out to the meadow path.

Mack's father had had guns at the ranch, a dozen fine shotguns some a hundred years old, including his beautiful doublebarrel Ithaca with a pheasant carved into the stock and hung above the mantel. Only one rifle was kept in the rafters of the bunkhouse, and to Mack's knowledge it had never been used. He tried to remember if it was still there, some 30-30 from Sears. There was one handgun, a little .22 in the kitchen drawer for snakes and the like. It was hard to find for the egg beaters and scotch tape. Mack himself had shot a lot of pheasants and waterfowl but never a swan, though there was a season. He'd never shot a deer and his father thought that phenomenon was no rite of passage in country where whitetail were tame as dogs. Now kneeling by his wounded friend, he held his great cup of Clay's great coffee and he wasn't sure it was going to go down.

"You want more cream in that coffee."

"It's perfect."

Clay said. "I shot a man once."

"You did not."

"Mack, I did." Clay closed his eyes while he talked. He had folded his arms over his chest.

"And when was this."

"At the home place in Sudman."

"Your dad's place."

"Right."

"Who'd you shoot?"

"A thief, some guy named Curlbeaker. He and his brother worked the whole area we found out; they had a state road trailer and they were stealing tractors and ATVs, anything left out in the yard."

"You blasted him with buckshot one night."

"I did. Three in the morning or so, four, and when I came out of the house, he climbed down from our old John Deere and ran for the road where the truck was waiting and I shot once at about thirty yards and he went down and rolled and started screaming and his brother took off trailer and all. They caught him south of Rock Springs; he'd run out of gas."

"What happened to the one you shot?"

"He was blood from knee to shoulder, completely peppered and the ass shot out of his pants. He was a week in the hospital and then he sued us." Clay opened his eyes and laughed. "But then he and all of the Curlbeakers disappeared, off to warmer country is my bet. But there's still number-six pheasant shot in that guy's backside."

"How'd you feel about it?"

"I felt I should have felt better. Everybody said, good deal, like that, but I didn't care for it. I'd do it again in the middle of the night on my own place or for my people, but I don't care for it, Mack. It's the way we're made." Clay looked hard at Mack. "This guy of yours up here, he did some things to the women for which he's answered. I heard them talking while you were gone, and that's why I was out there with my gun. You did the right thing, but it isn't going to be easy, none of it. Right, but not easy. I'll stand witness if it comes to that."

"I've got one more thing," Mack told Clay, and he rose and retrieved his daypack with the material he'd taken from the crash site. He mounted Buddy once again and trotted up to Canby's body. The day was done. He dropped to the ground and tied the pack to Canby's belt and then he covered the body with his yellow poncho weighing down the corners with round rocks. He stood directly and marched up to the trees at the upper end of the meadow and up the trail and there he saw that the other man was gone. He would have reclaimed his horse and crossed back into the mountains by now. Okay. Mack felt his heart pounding and he dropped his head. Everything was gone.

On the way down the meadow, he heard the medical helicopter chuffing and just the faint and strange flutter hurt his chest. He walked Buddy around the back of the hunters' tent and clipped both horses to the rope line back in the trees and then Mack walked out into the meadow and waved his hat, pointing at the flat spot and then backing up as the machine descended. The helicopter settled and changed the whole place. Even as it idled, the noise was terrific. There were two medics aboard; one was the pilot.

"I'm going to hike out tonight." Mack knelt by Clay. He had to speak loudly.

"You still look a little cooked."

"No, I'm okay. I want to say goodbye to Vonnie; I've got to." He stood up. "I don't know when I'll see her again."

"You're going to want your pack," Clay said, pointing.

"Right. We left two sleeping bags in the trees there above the west point of Valentine too."

"I'll arrange with Bluebride to have them picked up before the end of the month."

"Thanks." Mack shook the young man's hand. "You're a good friend, Clay."

"Okay then."

One medic with his big gray box knelt by Clay and started to scissor off the temporary bandages. The other came to Mack and yelled in his ear, "Who's shooting?"

"The shooting's done," Mack said. "One dead above here and one injured off on his own." He pointed. "Just get Clay to town." The man nodded and turned to Clay.

Mack crossed the grassy open, his shadow reaching ten feet as it led him through the wildflowers and sage in the last light of the afternoon. The sun was weak light, and the chill was general headed for a real freeze. The watery yellow day wanted to break his heart. The season had foundered and each day was now a brave imitation of the day before. In September the year fell away and in the car you'd get a late baseball game on the radio as you drove to town sounding like it was coming from another planet, the static and the crowd noise and the announcers trying to fend off the fall shadows. He found the trail and went down to the timber fence that marked the wilderness, and he crawled up the step-stile there, hands and feet, standing for a moment on the top, and then he eased down and was out of the woods. Now it was the three long gentle hills around through the state forest. He was run with thoughts. When they'd hiked in, he anticipated this walk in a different way. It was always delicious coming out, dirty and tired and they were always talking, going over the fish they'd caught, the whole trip. On such days his father always said, "Being dirty, like being hungry, are fine things that need earning. We did that, so let's go wash up and eat." He taught Mack never to waste being hungry but to use it like an instrument, and they'd eaten many fine steaks in the big roadhouses at the edge of the western towns when they'd come down from the hills. "Let's use this right"— Mack had said that every year to Vonnie; they both knew that they'd have steaks and cold drinks from the day-out cooler, a celebration and one last night camped near the cars above the world. One year he'd brought champagne which had been a mistake, their heads keeping them slow until noon the next day, and he had said first, "I am flat out allergic to that beverage."

Now he didn't know. He guessed Vonnie would take Amy to the clinic in Dubois or Lander or all the way to Jackson for the big doctors. Walking felt good to him now, but he still felt like he was going to lose it, cough up Clay's coffee. It wasn't the sight of the dead man but the fear as he'd lifted the rifle that was still working in him. He bent to his knees again and waited, and then he saw something up off the trail and it moved. A moose, and then he looked again and it was one of Bluebride's red steers, eyeing him from the trees. "Oh boy," he said. "You've done it now. Come on. Let's go down. Whup whup. There's nothing to eat up here." The steer regarded Mack without moving. "Come come," he said. The beast stood. Mack backtracked the trail and stepped up to the animal from behind and even then the steer wouldn't move. He could see Bluebride's brand, the B with three bulbs, there on his side. "Go go go," Mack said, finally putting his hand on the flank and the animal started and pushed reluctantly down toward the dirt path. "Whup, whup," he said, "I'm not going to push you all the way." He flat-handed the steer's rump softly, and finally the beast trotted ahead as if he'd suddenly figured out the game. Mack smiled and it was funny how a big animal helped. His stomach would be okay. He'd get down and do the next thing. The woods were dark through the last level section with the trail here broad as a sidewalk.

"Let's go," he said, and the lone steer stepped heavily down and out into the meadow of the trailhead as if carrying the night and all the stars on its old back. In the changed light of the open field, the steer trotted ahead, a hundred yards and then two, as if it'd seen the four tiny distant lights of the Crowheart store, as Mack had, and knew exactly where it should go.

Vonnie's car was still there by his, all the doors open and Amy was lying in the backseat under the plaid car blanket. Vonnie had the trunk open and was changing clothes there, buttoning a clean shirt when he came up. He went by her, not speaking, and opened his old blue truck wishing he had a dog now, somebody to jump up in and be happy to be there. He threw his pack on the passenger floor. Out across the eastern prairie lights were coming on at the various ranch outposts, the planet under transition. Mack knelt on the ground and pulled his cooler from under the truck and lifted it onto the tailgate. It was always like opening a treasure chest, but not tonight.

"You want a beer," he said to Vonnie.

"I don't know," she said. "When Amy feels better, we're going out." She came over to where he stood looking in at the wrapped steaks, the cold beer and root beer, the tomatoes in the tray. His lump of dry ice was just about gone. "Same old," she said. "Except for the root beer."

"It's awful good. There's no compromise in root beer," he said. "I'm going to start a fire and stay up. I've got no reason to hurry down to that town."

"Gimme one," she said. He extracted a tall Pacifico from the cooler and opened it with his knife. He went up to the edge of the trees and found a pile of branches from the last guys and he started a small fire and fed it up. Vonnie went and checked the girl and then walked over.

"Do you need my kit?" he asked. "The first aid."

"No, we'll go to the hospital."

"See the cops."

"Yes, the cops."

"I shot that guy at five minutes to five, if they want to know. I'll be here and then to my apartment by noon tomorrow. It's going to freeze up here, so they can get him tomorrow. It's my yellow poncho just below the creek."

"I'm sorry, Mack."

"Oh shit," he said. "I'm sorry he hurt you. Sorry for the trip. Just sorry."

She stood above him, arms folded, holding her beer with her shirtsleeve. "Don't," she said.

"I'm going to get a dog," he said.

"You should. Can you have one in that apartment?"

"There's twenty," he said. "Besides I'm going to move back onto the ranch. If I'm broke, I should be broke in the right place anyhow."

"That's a good idea. What will you get?"

"An Aussie, probably. Somebody who can read Keats. I may take a few guests next spring, summer."

"Really."

"I know how to do it."

"I know you do. You know some stories."

"I was thinking of having a week or two only kids."

She looked at him funny and said, "Goddamn cold beer." Vonnie started to cry standing there, and he moved and held her.

"Goddamned last trip," he said. "I'm sorry." She put her arms around him in the firelight, sobbing, and he felt her mouth on his neck saying something he could barely hear.

There was a noise he couldn't place which then became the sound of a vehicle approaching from below.

"Somebody's coming. It might be the sheriff now," he said.

"That would be good."

His fire was right and he stood and ran a finger into his coin pocket. "Here's your ring," he said.

Suddenly they were in the high beams as the big truck

mounted the trailhead and drove up. It looked like the sheriff a minute but became a big red Hummer with chrome wheels and a rack of lamps like a freight train.

"It's Kent," Mack said, letting Vonnie go. "He's got some cars." The wake of dust rose up when the truck stopped and came over them as Kent climbed down. He hadn't turned off his headlights. He came forward in big strides in another million-dollar shirt, crosshatched with blue and green.

"Yvonne," he said. "Where the hell have you been?"

"I'm right here," she said. "The phone went dead and we've had some trouble."

"God damn you, Mack," Kent said. "You pissant."

"You're starting right in," Mack said.

"I've had two hours to think about it."

"I've had a year," Mack said.

"Did you get Yarnell's treasure?" Kent said.

Mack eyed the man in the deep twilight. It was a city face, layered with shallow intrigues, business, profit. It was without question a notable and beautiful shirt. He wondered what made Kent work. He'd only now understood what worked for himself. Mack shook his head.

"I think you did," Kent said.

"There's my pack," Mack told the man. "Just take it."

"We will," he said, and he retrieved Mack's pack. "Charley outsmarted the agency and he outsmarted you, but that's not really very hard."

Kent was smiling. Now he pointed to where Amy sat in Vonnie's dark car. "Who's that?" Kent said.

"We've had some trouble," Vonnie said again.

"It's okay now," Mack told him. "We're all safe. You're here."

Then Kent went back to the big vehicle and reached under the seat and came back with a beautiful silver handgun, a .44 with an eight-inch barrel and he walked past Vonnie and Mack and lifted the pistol with both hands and shot the door of Mack's truck dead center.

Amy screamed.

"Fuck!" Mack said. The explosion was still in the air. "Fuck! Are you fucking crazy?"

"Let's go, Yvonne."

"I've got to see to the girl."

"Bring her. We'll get your car on the weekend." Kent was back at the Hummer.

"You goddamn idiot," Mack said. "You fucking"—he lost a word—"solicitor." He hung his head a moment and then walked over to where Kent sat up in the driver's seat. His tinted window was up. "This is state land. I didn't shoot your car. I broke the windshield with a tire iron and I was drunk and I paid for it and spent some weeks in jail. This doesn't make us even. This doesn't do anything except fuck my truck up. I'll have rust till Sunday with that hole."

"Get in!" Kent yelled at Vonnie. "Get over here!" She was helping Amy.

"We can't, Kent. I'll drive down. We're okay now."

Mack went to Vonnie at her car. "It was the ranch, that money. That's why I took Yarnell's gig." He walked past her to the fire and tended it. Her beer bottle stood there in the dirt. He'd pulled himself in as far as he could. "Go to the hospital," he said to her across the space.

Kent had backed the giant car around and his high beams shot out into space. Then Mack snapped. He felt it as a snap under his breastbone and the day rose up in him and he saw the young rider explode backward off that horse, and Mack's throat closed. He ran at Kent's red vehicle.

"Mack," Vonnie said. "Oh God."

Now he had a river rock in his hand, big as a grapefruit, and still running he raised it and swung it with all his force against Kent's window. It bounced off, ricocheting back to the ground, stinging Mack's hand. "Shit!"

Kent jolted forward, the beast roaring down the rocky two-track fifty yards and stopping again, ten red lights in the teeming dust.

"He's got that gun," Vonnie said. But Mack had the rock again and was running down. "Mack!" The Hummer gunned and bounced away, too fast, and over the hill, only a glow now in the frigid night. Mack dropped the rock and still ran. From the ridge he saw the dotted lights descend the trailhead road. At one point the brakelights flared, and Mack saw Kent swerve to avoid the steer. He stood, his breath baggy plumes shooting into the air. He hated to run and he had to do it. The stars were out complete and in the open sky he saw the smoky run of the Milky Way all the way to Canada. Back at the trailhead both women sat in Vonnie's closed car. It was running and she rolled the window down.

Vonnie's face was funny, drained. "I can't drive," she said. "I thought I could. Just take us down." He went to the creek with the bucket from the bed of his truck and extinguished the coals of his fire. Mack grabbed his pack, closed up his vehicle. He had the women sit in the back of Vonnie's Lexus under the blanket, and carefully backed the new car and started down to the highway.

They went south to Lander. The passed the Crowheart store, the yard light and the porch light. "They've got Dreamsicles in the front freezer," he said. "I like a Dreamsicle. They're hard to find." The expanse of the Indian reservation was dark. From time to time they passed a ranch yard with a light showing the two trucks and the basketball pole.

"You knew I was looking for Yarnell's plane or whatever?" Mack said.

"Let's not talk, Mack. You don't know what you're doing half the time. Let's not talk."

Ten minutes later Vonnie said. "You got a story? The one about Hiram and Amateur?"

"I do," he began. "Now there was a man who was misunderstood." They seemed far away from the mountains in the night now and he told the story on the deserted highway.

In the story tonight Mack said that Hiram Corazon worked with the wild geese while guarding the love he felt in his heart for Lucinda Amateur. Mack drove and talked in the quiet car, as if speaking to the fields and the dark ranches. There was an evil plot at the sewing works, he said, and the evil plot was to use less goose down in the comforters. It was a kind of pleasure for Mack to say words as the story opened. Very soon in his story the greedy assistant director of the comforter institute got involved in an involved plot, a plot with seven layers and all of them secret, the whispers of which were overheard by the geese themselves, who had no end of trouble making their story clear to Hiram because of the language barrier. They called and whispered but they spoke as geese and he could only understand a part at a time. Slowly, this took miles in the driving, Hiram began to understand what the geese were saying, and once he saw what was going on, he told the townsfolk, but then was not believed, at all, and was shunned from the village and considered crazy and dangerous and he wandered in the forest listening for a beating heart.

Vonnie interrupted here and said, "We found his canoe one time."

"It's still in the mountains, the only canoe in the Winds." Mack could hear in his voice how tired he was. He talked and he felt himself slip away from the story as he spoke, the words still falling, and he thought of Chester and the angle of the man's neck in the sharp mountain sunlight. He remembered his friend saying once, "Mack, you got to cowboy longer than most of us. You're the only guy who has a shot at going back to it. "

He had stopped telling the story and they drove in silence until Amy said, "What about Lucinda?"

"That's it," Mack said. And he told of Hiram trying to figure out a way to tell his own true love of the evil plot, and he finally clarified the entire intrigue to Lucinda in secret code that he embedded in the songs he sang outside her window after her guardians had gone to sleep in their thick down comforters.

"Like what?" Vonnie asked.

"Like secret code embedded in a musical number," he said. "You're a music major. You understand. Anyway, Hiram had learned to play the guitar and he stood below her window in the proper manner. Every night was serenade. He sang the songs a phrase at a time, some of the phrases drawn from Shelley and some from Keats."

Mack knew the dark country through which he drove the women. He knew they were asleep, but still he talked, telling the story to himself. Hiram Corazon played the guitar though he had never studied music. The story had sharp and telling comparisons between the pure comforters and the adulterated blankets that were not only not warm but itched mercilessly. "They were itch-i-genic," Mack said.

"That's not a word," Vonnie said. It had been almost an hour, and they were entering the western town.

"It's a word and a condition. Those comforters were used for rhinoceros saddles. They didn't itch those animals."

Amy had been asleep and said, "Rhinoceros saddles."

"The end," Mack said. "There's a good story."

At the ER in Lander, he got a wheelchair and helped Amy inside. Vonnie went to the counter. The nurse called the doctor and the police. It was very strange to be indoors, for all of them, and Mack said, as they waited, "They've got this place about lighted up." The magazines lay about on the plastic tables and for some reason they looked evil to him. Mack went to the men's and washed his hands twice with the powerful soap and then his face and up into his hair, drying himself with the coarse paper towels and then mopping up the sink. He sat down to wait. It was ten-thirty.

It took all night. Mack talked to the police for an hour in a borrowed office and then he went over to the station with the deputy, a guy named Bradham, and he was there drinking terrible coffee and sorting it all out for two hours. He filled out the report and signed four papers, one of which promised he wouldn't leave the state. There were examinations and tests, and they found a deep plum bruise below Mack's elbow that he could not remember receiving, and a nurse swabbed his ears and put a drop of something in each one so they sizzled a minute and then she gave him a little white tube of the stuff. Mack brought in the clothes kit from Vonnie's trunk and she came back eventually in her moccasins and an orange plaid pair of dorm pants that he remembered and a UNC sweatshirt with an old red scarf she'd had forever, and she folded a set of clothes in Amy's room. They were keeping her a day, and her parents were coming from Missoula. She was awake and looking good, sort of happy in fact, when they went in to see her.

"I'm okay," she said, "but I'm tired. I can get through this. Your name is Mack," she said.

"Howdy."

"So the guy only listened to people's hearts trying to find his own?"

"That's it."

"And they thought he was a cannibal for it?"

"He scared them in their campsites," Mack said. "He's still up there in the Winds searching."

"Jeez," she said. "It's a good story."

"Just so your parents know," Mack said. "You went in at Dubois and came out at Cold Creek trailhead and here's this, my phone number if they want to talk to me." Mack left the room a minute so Vonnie could speak to the young woman. He went out and scraped her windshield, the first time he'd done such a thing this season. It was the first stroke of winter. He brought the car up under the ER entry a minute later and Vonnie got in.

"I thought they'd keep you," he said. He put her hand on his shoulder.

"We got beat up. It was the worst thing I've ever had, but they were spaced out and I tricked them both." Her jaw was set hard, and her eyes were clear and cold. "I'm tired, but okay. You tracked me down, right?"

"I found your fly rod, your ring."

"Needle in a haystack."

"Our haystack."

She let it pass and said, "You want to drive back and get your truck?"

"Yeah, we can do that. We better before it gets snowed in. But I want to get a big fry first since we're in town."

"Some eggs," she said.

"A spinach omelette," he said, "with rye toast and potatoes and maybe a little piece of steak. Something that uses the whole plate."

"I know a place," she said.

"Show the way," he said. "I've got the money with me."

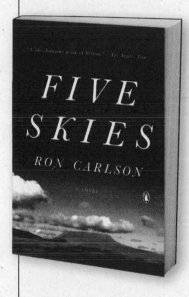